"Nicky likes and trusts you. I've checked your qualifications and employment record and I believe you are the best person to help him."

He exhaled heavily when she continued to shake her head. "I will pay you generously."

Instead of replying, she turned away from him and walked across the room to stare out of the window. Marco roamed his eyes over her, admiring the way her jeans molded to her pert derriere. She had restrained her hair in a braid, and he longed to untie it and sink his hands into her riotous curls while he covered her mouth with his.

He swore beneath his breath as he felt his body's predictable response to his erotic thoughts. Somehow he would have to ignore his desire for Leah. "There is nothing I will not do for my son," he said deeply. "Name your price."

She swung around to face him and hugged her arms around her slender body. Marco had the odd sense that she was trying to stop herself from falling apart.

"My price is marriage. Marry me before the end of the month and I will do my best to help Nicky."

Chantelle Shaw lives on the Kent coast and thinks up her stories while walking on the beach. She has been married for over thirty years and has six children. Her love affair with reading and writing Harlequin stories began as a teenager, and her first book was published in 2006. She likes strong-willed, slightly unusual characters. Chantelle also loves gardening, walking and wine.

Books by Chantelle Shaw

Harlequin Presents

Acquired by Her Greek Boss
Hired for Romano's Pleasure
The Virgin's Sicilian Protector
Reunited by a Shock Pregnancy
Wed for the Spaniard's Redemption
Proof of Their Forbidden Night

Secret Heirs of Billionaires

Wed for His Secret Heir

Wedlocked!

Trapped by Vialli's Vows

Bought by the Brazilian

Mistress of His Revenge
Master of Her Innocence

The Saunderson Legacy

The Secret He Must Claim
The Throne He Must Take

Visit the Author Profile page
at Harlequin.com for more titles.

Chantelle Shaw

HER WEDDING NIGHT NEGOTIATION

PAPL
DISCARDED

HARLEQUIN
PRESENTS

HARLEQUIN®
PRESENTS®

Recycling programs
for this product may
not exist in your area.

ISBN-13: 978-1-335-14871-1

Her Wedding Night Negotiation

Copyright © 2020 by Chantelle Shaw

All rights reserved. No part of this book may be used or reproduced in
any manner whatsoever without written permission except in the case of
brief quotations embodied in critical articles and reviews.

This is a work of fiction. Names, characters, places and incidents
are either the product of the author's imagination or are used fictitiously.
Any resemblance to actual persons, living or dead, businesses,
companies, events or locales is entirely coincidental.

This edition published by arrangement with Harlequin Books S.A.

For questions and comments about the quality of this book,
please contact us at CustomerService@Harlequin.com.

Harlequin Enterprises ULC
22 Adelaide St. West, 40th Floor
Toronto, Ontario M5H 4E3, Canada
www.Harlequin.com

Printed in U.S.A.

HER WEDDING NIGHT NEGOTIATION

CHAPTER ONE

MARCO DE VALLE HATED WEDDINGS. Hated all the fuss that was deemed a necessary part of the fiasco when two people publicly made promises that one or both of them probably would not keep.

He wished he could miss his half-brother's nuptials and fly home to Capri with his young son tonight. But to please his mother—although he did not know why he bothered to try, when it had been obvious for years that he was not her favourite offspring—he had agreed to attend James's wedding to his drippy fiancée.

Marco's mother was only keen for him to be at the ceremony tomorrow because his presence was bound to attract media interest, and a photograph of the wedding would perhaps appear in a celebrity magazine, he thought cynically.

The wedding rehearsal should have started twenty minutes ago but James was late. Stifling his impatience, Marco leaned against a pillar in a shadowy recess at the back of the private chapel, which belonged to the Nancarrow estate, and studied the bride, who was standing at the front of the nave.

His first impression of Leah Ashbourne when he'd met her earlier in the day had been that he had never seen a woman with such pale skin or such terrible dress sense. Her white blouse was buttoned up to her throat and her navy skirt fell to several inches below her knees. She wore her reddish-brown hair in a no-nonsense braid that hung between her shoulder blades and she could have passed for a nun—or Mary Poppins.

Her personality seemed to be as unexciting as her appearance, although Marco had been intrigued by the flush of rose-pink that had spread across her cheeks as she'd mumbled a greeting when James had introduced them. It had been a long time since he'd seen a woman blush. Marco had revised his opinion of Leah as plain at that point, acknowledging that she was actually very pretty, albeit not his type. He liked sexually confident women who understood that he wasn't interested in commitment and would never, ever offer them marriage. Once had been enough.

He glanced at his watch and cursed beneath his breath. In an hour it would be Nicky's bedtime and Marco had wanted to spend some time with his son. He already felt guilty that he'd been called away on an urgent business trip which had meant him leaving Nicky behind at Nancarrow Hall with the nanny for the past week.

Guilt played a big part in his relationship with Nicky, he acknowledged with a deep sigh. The psychotherapist who had been working with the little boy insisted that a five-year-old did not have the emotional capacity to blame Marco for the accident in which Nicky's mother had died. But Marco blamed himself. He had failed Nicky in the past, and he was failing him now because he could not seem to find a way to connect with his traumatised son.

Where the hell was James?

Marco saw Leah check her phone, and her shoulders slump. She looked a forlorn figure as she waited at the altar for her bridegroom, but he reminded himself it wasn't up to him to explain that James was not the Prince Charming she clearly believed he was.

His thoughts returned to his son. He'd bought a toy sports car—a model of his own Ferrari—for Nicky, and he was looking forward to watching him open the gift. Perhaps the little boy would give one of his rare smiles.

Marco refused to waste any more time waiting for the wedding rehearsal to begin and he stepped out of the recess into the main part of the chapel.

'Is there *still* no sign of the bridegroom?' The vicar smiled sympathetically at Leah.

'I can't imagine what has happened to James,' she said, checking her phone again. 'He was going to Padstow to pick up a few last-minute things for our honeymoon, but he promised he would be back by six-thirty for the wedding rehearsal.'

There was no message from her fiancé to explain why he was delayed, but Leah remembered how James had driven at a snail's pace along the narrow Cornish lanes on the way to Nancarrow Hall a week ago. He was certainly not a daredevil, and she reassured herself that if he'd had an accident the emergency services would have alerted his parents. It was more likely that he'd lost track of the time, which was not unusual.

James tended to daydream, and he was hopelessly disorganised. Sometimes Leah felt more like his nanny than his partner, and since she'd arrived at Nancarrow Hall and met his parents she'd realised that they were overlyprotective of James. She suspected that he had been cossetted his whole life. But he was amiable, and easy-going, and their relationship had none of the drama and tension that Leah remembered from her childhood, when her mother had lurched from one disastrous love affair to another.

They had only been dating for six months, but she'd pushed away her doubts that their courtship had not been long enough for her to be certain she wanted to spend the rest of her life with James Fletcher. He had been in a strange mood since they had arrived at his family's gothic mansion on the edge of Bodmin Moor, but surely it was natural that they were both experiencing pre-wedding nerves.

Leah's conscience pricked. She knew that she should have told James about the money she had been left by her grandmother. But she'd been worried that the stipulation in Grandma Grace's will that she must be married before she could claim her inheritance might complicate her relationship with James. She loved him. She *did*.

Leah refused to listen to the voice of her conscience, which warned her that she was rushing into marriage because she craved the kind of settled life that she'd never known during her chaotic childhood.

'I have an appointment with the Bishop later this evening,' the vicar said. 'We will have to start the rehearsal without James. Perhaps someone can stand in for him until he gets here?'

He surveyed the group of people assembled in the private chapel. It was a small wedding with only forty guests. Thirty-nine of them were friends and family of the groom.

Leah directed a questioning look at Amy, her best friend from university and bridesmaid. Amy was an old school friend of James and it was she who had introduced him to Leah at a party. Leah had been flattered by his attention. She considered herself no more than averagely attractive and she'd assumed that good-looking, public-school-educated James was out of her league.

She had been drawn to the sense of security he represented. Once they were married they planned to move out of London and buy a little cottage with roses growing around the front door, and in time they would have two children and a dog. Other women might yearn for riches, designer clothes and dazzling jewels, but Leah's dream was a family.

Amy gave a shrug as an awkward silence followed the vicar's request for a stand-in bridegroom.

'I'm sure there must be a good reason why James is late.'

Davina, the ultra-efficient wedding planner spoke

in an oddly thick voice, and she looked as though she had been crying.

'Ideally we need someone who doesn't have a prominent role in the wedding ceremony to act as the groom.'

'I'll take James's place.'

The deep voice laced with a sexy accent came from the back of the chapel.

Leah stiffened and felt a peculiar sensation, as if her stomach had swooped down to her toes. That voice could only belong to Marco De Valle, James's Italian half-brother. Earlier in the day she had watched a tall, dark-haired man climb out of a sleek silver sports car and inexplicably her stomach had done the same swooping thing it was doing now.

When the stranger had walked into the drawing room and James had introduced him Leah had felt overwhelmed by Marco's magnetism. His supreme self-assurance gave him a presence that made everything and everyone around him fade to grey. She had darted a glance at Marco's face before hastily dropping her gaze, feeling as flustered and tongue-tied as a teenager who had just met her celebrity idol. Her blood had pounded in her ears as she'd mumbled a greeting.

That brief look had revealed that the half-brothers bore no resemblance to each other. James, with his blond hair and clean-cut image, was boyishly handsome. He had done some modelling work and appeared on the front covers of several glossy magazines of the kind which featured articles about stately homes and Royal Ascot.

The kind of publication that might have a photo of Marco De Valle on its front cover would be magazines about extreme sports or how to survive if you were stranded in the Amazonian jungle, Leah thought wryly. There was something untamed about him, and she sensed that he lived by his own rules and did not care a jot what others thought of him.

That feeling had been reinforced when she'd watched him from her bedroom window, striding across the moors—an imposing figure with his black coat swirling in the wind and his hair blown back from his face.

James had told her that the jagged scar on Marco's face was the result of a terrible accident in which his wife had been killed, leaving his five-year-old son motherless. Poor Nicky. The little boy was clearly still disturbed by the tragedy, and he rarely spoke or smiled. It was obvious to Leah that, having lost his mother, he needed to be with his father as much as possible, but James had said that Marco often left Nicky at Nancarrow Hall while he went abroad.

Perhaps Marco's absences were unavoidable, but having grown up never feeling that she was her mother's main priority, Leah had felt her heart go out to Nicky. His big brown eyes reminded her poignantly of her little brother, who had died when he was not much older than Nicky. There was not a day when Leah did not think of Sammy, and spending time with Nicky during the past week, while James had been busy, had been bittersweet.

Her thoughts scattered now, as she watched Marco

stroll down the aisle towards her, and she was dismayed when her pulse quickened in an unbidden response to him.

She noticed that his scar sliced down his cheek from just beneath his right eye to the corner of his mouth, making his top lip curl slightly and giving him a permanently cynical expression that was mirrored in his wintry grey eyes. On any other man the scar might have been regarded as a disfigurement, but it merely accentuated Marco's raw masculinity.

'Handsome' did not come close to describing his chiselled features: razor-sharp cheekbones and a square, determined jaw shaded with dark stubble. Above that sullen, sexy mouth was a strong nose rising to meet heavy dark brows. His hair was the same shade of almost black, overlong and dishevelled, as though he had just left a lover's bed after a night of passion.

Where that last thought had come from Leah had no idea, but the picture in her mind of Marco's naked body sprawled on satin sheets did nothing to help her already shaky composure.

She had never even seen a naked man before.

Other than on a no-holds-barred television dating show which, to Leah's mind, had been completely unromantic.

Marco moved with the silence and speed of a panther stalking its prey. Before Leah had time to collect her wits he was standing beside her. Her mouth dried as she forced herself to meet his sardonic gaze and she wondered if he heard her heart as it collided with her ribs. The jolt of awareness was unlike anything she'd ever felt before.

Not even for James. whispered her conscience, which seemed hell-bent on causing trouble.

'You don't have to do this,' she told Marco stiffly. 'I'm sure James will be here any minute now.'

'Your confidence in my brother is admirable,' he drawled, 'but James is as bad at time-keeping as he is at holding down a job.'

'It wasn't *his* fault he was sacked from the art gallery.' Leah sprang to her fiancé's defence. 'It was unfortunate that his alarm failed to go off and he overslept. He was only late for work a few times.'

'Well, I'm not prepared to wait any longer for him to show up.' Marco's gaze narrowed on Leah's flushed face. 'I understand you have only known my brother for a matter of months? If you'd like my advice, it is that you should postpone the wedding until you're certain that you are both ready for marriage.'

'I *don't* want your advice, thank you,' she snapped with icy politeness.

His grey eyes gleamed. 'The little mouse has a temper?' he said softly. 'Perhaps you are not as uninteresting as I thought when James introduced us.'

He ignored her furious gasp and turned to speak to the wedding planner.

'Reverend Tregarth is right. We should push on with the rehearsal without James. My housekeeper is planning to serve a buffet dinner this evening to allow the kitchen staff time to start preparing the wedding food for tomorrow.'

Leah saw Davina nod meekly. Marco had an air of authority and obviously expected other people to accept his leadership. But she was puzzled that he had spoken of *his* housekeeper. Surely the staff were employed by James's parents, whom she assumed were the owners of Nancarrow Hall? James had said that Marco lived mainly in Italy, where he headed De Valle Caffè—a world-famous coffee company and coffee-house chain.

The wedding planner opened the folder she was holding, entitled *Fletcher/Ashbourne Wedding 21st July.* 'We'll start without James and I can fill him in on what he needs to know later. As all the guests are here, I'll ask everyone to stand in their correct places while we run through the order of service.'

The vicar stood on the chancel steps as Davina directed people to their places.

'The groom and best man will stand on the right side of the chapel. The bridesmaid and the bride's family will be on the left side. But it might be better if the groom's friends and relatives fill the pews on both sides of the nave,' the wedding planner said hurriedly, realising that Leah's side of the chapel would be empty apart from Amy. 'And the bride and groom will stand facing the minister.'

As Leah moved into place she glanced over her shoulder, hoping to see James rushing through the doorway. She noticed a satisfied expression on his mother's face and guessed that Olivia Fletcher would not be disappointed if James had changed his mind and called off the wedding. Olivia had more airs and graces than royalty, and had made it plain that she believed her youngest son was marrying beneath him.

'It's *such* a shame your mother is on an around-the-world cruise and won't be able to share your big day,' Olivia had said with fake sincerity when Leah had explained that her father was dead, and her mother wouldn't be attending the wedding.

Her mother being on a cruise had been a blatant but necessary lie. Leah shuddered at the idea of her mum staggering into the church and behaving outrageously, as Tori had done many times in the past. She had even turned up drunk to Leah's university graduation ceremony and ruined what should have been a proud day.

James had only met Tori once. Leah had invited him round early one Saturday morning, when her mum was usually still sober. The meeting had gone without incident, although Leah had quickly invented an excuse when James had suggested they all go to the pub for lunch.

During James's visit Leah had seen her mum almost as she'd remembered her from long ago: intelligent and articulate with a hint of the great beauty she had once had in her smile. But when she'd gone into the kitchen to make a cup of tea she had found a bottle of vodka that Tori had hidden in the cupboard under the sink. She hadn't had a chance to pour the vodka away, and she knew that Tori would have finished the bottle by that evening and visited the local supermarket to buy more.

Leah had felt too embarrassed to tell James about her mother's drink problem. She'd spent her childhood wishing that her mum was 'normal', like other parents. It hadn't been so bad when they'd lived abroad in a commune, with Tori's artist friends. But when Leah was twelve they had moved back to England.

She cringed at memories of her mum attending school functions drunk and talking too loudly, attracting attention. Once at a prize-giving ceremony Tori had flirted with the headmaster and then thrown up in the school hall in front of everyone. From then on Leah had never invited Tori to school events, but that hadn't stopped the other kids' taunts that her mum was 'an alky'.

After the wedding she would explain to James that her mum was what was termed a 'functioning alcoholic'. Somehow Tori managed to hold down her job as a bookkeeper with a building firm, but her heavy drinking every weekend was destroying her health. Leah was sure James would be supportive of her intention to use some of her inheritance to pay for specialist treatment for her mum.

Where was he?

She started to turn her head towards the back of the chapel, hoping to see that James had arrived, but her gaze snagged on Marco's enigmatic grey eyes. She estimated that he must be three or four inches over six feet tall, as she had to angle her neck to look at him, and his chiselled features had a peculiar effect on her pulse. From where she was standing, she couldn't see his scar, and her breath caught in her throat as she studied the sculpted perfection of his bone structure. He was beautiful in a powerfully masculine way.

She could not stop staring at his face and he lifted one dark brow mockingly, as if he was aware that she was fascinated by him. Blushing hotly, Leah jerked her eyes towards the front of the chapel. She was trembling. *Not* because she was fiercely aware of Marco, she assured herself, but because she was angry at his arrogance when he had said he thought she was uninteresting.

She forced herself to concentrate when the vicar spoke.

'At the beginning of the ceremony the bride and groom will turn to face each other and hold hands.'

Reluctantly Leah turned towards Marco, and her heart gave a jolt when he reached for her hands. She was about to tell him that it wasn't necessary to practise *every* detail of the wedding, but before she could speak he wrapped his strong fingers around hers, enveloping her small hands in his much bigger ones.

She inhaled swiftly as a sensation like an electrical current shot through her fingers and up her arms. Marco's touch was warm and firm, and she sensed inherent strength in his grasp. She stared down at their linked hands and noted how his darkly tanned skin contrasted with her milky paleness. Her traitorous mind imagined his fingers skimming over her naked body and curving around her breasts.

Swallowing hard, Leah raised her eyes to Marco's chest, where the top few buttons of his sky-blue shirt were undone, revealing a vee of tanned skin and a sprinkling of black hair. He smelled of soap and spice:

exotic notes of a bergamot and sandalwood cologne mixed with an indefinable scent that was raw male.

On the periphery of her mind she registered that the vicar was explaining how he would talk them through the ceremony rather than read through the entire wedding service word for word.

'You will want to save making your vows until the actual wedding, and to the right bridegroom,' he said, giving Leah a pointed look.

She felt guilty colour rise in her face. Had the vicar guessed that she was having inappropriate thoughts about the man who tomorrow would become her brother-in-law? How could her mind be so disloyal to James? Her reaction to Marco De Valle was inexplicable and inexcusable.

She tried to withdraw her hands from Marco's, but he tightened his fingers and stroked his thumb lightly back and forth over the pulse beating erratically in her wrist. Perhaps it was meant to be a soothing gesture, but it had the opposite effect, making Leah's heart pound so hard that she was surprised it wasn't visible beneath her shirt.

'After the declarations and the vows and the exchange of rings, the congregation will be seated while the bride, groom and witnesses accompany me into the vestry,' the vicar explained. 'Once the register has been signed, the newly married couple will return to stand at the altar rail, and I will invite the groom to kiss his bride.'

Leah's eyes jerked to Marco's face and she stared at his sensual mouth as he lowered his head towards her. Her heart lurched. He *wouldn't*! He *couldn't* mean to kiss her.

It must be shock that was keeping her feet welded to the floor. She did *not* want Marco to claim her mouth with his, she assured herself.

His dark head came closer and she felt the hard glitter in his eyes evoke a wild heat inside her. He filled her vision, and when her eyelashes swept down she could still see his chiselled features as though they were imprinted on her retinas.

The air around them seemed to tremble and Leah could hardly breathe. They stood like that—close, but not close enough—for what felt like a lifetime. But it could only have been a few seconds before the spell that Marco had cast on her was shattered.

'Sorry I'm late!'

The voice from the back of the chapel jolted Leah to her senses. Her eyes flew open and she drew a shuddering breath. Marco had already straightened up. Perhaps she'd only imagined that he had been on the brink of kissing her. His eyes were hooded, and she could not read his expression.

With a low cry she snatched her hands out of his and ran down the aisle. 'James, where have you been? Why didn't you answer your phone when I called you?'

'The battery died.' James's eyes sidled away from Leah's. 'You know how I always forget to charge it.'

She bit her lip. 'We had to start the rehearsal without you…your brother offered to take your place,' she explained, when Marco walked up to her and James.

Leah had previously sensed the coolness between

the brothers, and now the temperature in the chapel seemed to drop by several degrees as the two men faced each other.

'I trust you will afford your bride the courtesy of turning up on time for your actual wedding tomorrow?' Marco said curtly.

'*You* are hardly the right person to give me advice on how to treat my bride,' James muttered. 'Your marriage lasted for just a year, and it's rumoured that your wife died trying to escape from you.'

Leah's eyes flew to Marco. She expected him to say something in his defence, but he stayed silent. His face might as well have been carved from the same unforgiving granite as the chapel walls, and his eyes were the dull, cold grey of a midwinter sky. The scar on his cheek was a stark white line ruining the perfection of his olive skin.

He was beautiful, and terrible, and Leah could not understand why he had such a devastating effect on her. She was shocked by her uncontrolled response to Marco. A knot of tension tightened in the pit of her stomach as she wondered if her mother had been overwhelmed by this same helpless fascination with a man every time she'd rushed headlong into a new relationship.

She was *not* going to make the same mistakes as her mother, Leah promised herself. Thank goodness she was marrying dear, *safe* James, she thought as she watched Marco stride out of the chapel.

CHAPTER TWO

THE REHEARSAL DINNER was already underway when Marco entered the orangery. A buffet was laid out on long tables and guests were helping themselves to food. He accepted a glass of wine from the butler, but he felt too wired to eat.

One reason for his lack of appetite was his increasing concern about his relationship with his son. It had been too much to hope that Nicky would be pleased to see him, he thought heavily. After the wedding rehearsal had finished he'd hurried back to the house so that he could see him, but even when he'd given the little boy his present Nicky had shown no emotion apart from the wariness in his eyes that felt like a knife through Marco's heart.

The truth, Marco acknowledged, was that he had felt awkward when he'd sat there on the nursery floor and sought to engage his son in pushing toy cars along a track. He did not remember his own father ever playing with *him* and he had no real idea how to be a good parent. Yes, he'd read numerous books on parenting,

but none of them had offered advice on how to win the
trust of a child who seemed afraid of his own father.

He raked his fingers through his hair as his thoughts
turned to the other reason for his black mood. He must
have suffered a temporary mental aberration in the
church when he'd almost kissed the bride-to-be. Marco
remembered Leah had looked as stunned as he had
felt by the chemistry that had blazed between them.

He'd told himself that her air of innocence must be
an illusion. It was inconceivable that she and James
were not lovers, seeing as they were about to marry.
However, according to his housekeeper, James and
his fiancée were *not* sharing a bedroom at Nancarrow Hall.

Marco had sensed a vulnerability in Leah as he'd
stood next to her in front of the altar. It was a place
he had vowed never to stand again after his disastrous experience of holy matrimony. These wedding
preparations were evoking bitter memories of Karin
and reminding Marco of why he would never trust a
woman again.

He glanced around the room and saw James standing at the bar with the wedding planner. They appeared to be having a casual conversation, but Marco
curled his lip sardonically. Nothing that happened at
Nancarrow Hall did not reach his ears. But what his
half-brother got up to was none of his business, he reminded himself. It was not up to *him* to tell the bride
of his suspicions about James.

Marco spotted Leah over by the window and shock
ricocheted through him as he took in her transforma-

tion from dowdy and dull to absolutely stunning. He barely recognised her. She had changed her boring skirt and blouse for a cocktail dress in a pale apricot shade that emphasised the colour of her hair—which, now that it was not tied up, Marco saw was a riot of glorious red curls. She had drawn the front sections back with clips, but feathery strands had escaped and now framed her heart-shaped face. The strapless dress left her slender shoulders bare, and the skirt was made of layers of a wispy material that floated around her legs when she walked.

From where Marco was standing, on the other side of the orangery, he could not see the colour of her eyes, but he knew they were a startling vivid green. She was beautiful, he thought as he took a long sip of his wine, savouring the full-bodied Barolo on his tongue. Leah was a quintessential English rose, with creamy skin and hair the colour of burnished copper.

When he'd stood beside her in the private chapel he'd noticed that her face and arms were covered with tiny freckles, and his fingers had itched to unbutton her shirt and see if that dusting of gold continued lower. She was petite, and had a slender figure, but her breasts were surprisingly full and firm. Marco knew instinctively that they would fit perfectly into his palms.

He swore beneath his breath as he felt his body respond to the erotic images in his mind, but he could not tear his eyes from her. He knew that her mouth would fit his as if it had been designed purely for his pleasure. But thank God his sanity had prevailed and he'd resisted the temptation to kiss her in the chapel.

He watched Leah step outside onto the terrace and fought the urge to follow her. This strong attraction he felt for her was unsettling, and he was glad he was returning to Capri immediately after the wedding tomorrow. *Dio!* Desiring his soon-to-be sister-in-law was an unforeseen inconvenience.

He swung away from the window and frowned as he saw the nanny approaching him. Stacey was teetering on high heels, and her dress had a plunging neckline that left little to the imagination.

'Is Nicolo asleep?'

Marco had a relaxed attitude to his staff, and he had invited Stacey to join the party after Nicky had fallen asleep. His son did not like being left alone at night, and the nanny was supposed to stay with him in the nursery until he'd nodded off.

'He didn't seem tired, so I thought you wouldn't mind if he stayed up a little later than usual.'

Stacey stepped closer to him and ran her fingers through her blonde hair in an artful gesture that Marco found irritating.

'It's way past Nicky's bedtime,' he said tersely.

'It isn't fair to make him stay in his room when he can hear people enjoying themselves.'

Stacey sounded petulant, and Marco was in no doubt that she had wanted to join the party rather than sit in the nursery with a five-year-old. He sighed.

Nicky's previous nanny had left suddenly, to care for her elderly father. While they were staying at Nancarrow Hall he had arranged this temporary nanny through an agency. Unfortunately Stacey was more interested in flirting with him than looking after his son.

When he returned to Italy he planned to interview applicants personally, and find a suitable nanny for Nicky. With luck—and the promise of an exceptionally generous salary—he would be able to appoint someone who was prepared to stay for a few years and give his son some much needed stability.

'Where *is* Nicky?' he demanded, scanning the room.

'He must have gone outside. God, that kid!' Stacey muttered. 'I told him to stay inside.'

Marco was already walking swiftly over to the French doors. The sun was sinking behind the row of hawthorn trees that marked the boundary between the Nancarrow estate and the moor. He shaded his eyes against the golden rays as he stared across the wide expanse of lawn. An icy hand clutched his heart when he spotted a small figure with a mop of black curls down by the lake.

Nicky had climbed onto the wooden jetty where a rowboat was tied up. He was running to the far end of the jetty and peering into the water. Marco knew that the lake was deep, and well-stocked with carp and perch, and guessed that Nicky must be watching the fish.

'Nicky!'

It was unlikely that his voice would carry the length of the garden, Marco realised as he sprinted across the terrace and down the steps. Everything seemed to happen in slow motion. He watched his son lean over too far and topple into the water.

'Madre di Dio!'

He ran faster, his heart pounding with fear.

A figure in an apricot-coloured dress was some way in front of him, hurtling towards the lake. Leah. She kicked off her shoes and tore along the jetty. Without hesitating, she plunged into the water where Nicky had fallen in.

Marco imagined his son caught in the thick weeds that grew in the lake, choking for breath. How long would it take a child to drown?

His feet pounded on the wooden jetty and relief almost made his knees buckle as Leah surfaced, holding Nicky.

'It's all right, sweetheart, I've got you. Hold on tightly around my neck,' she instructed as she swam towards the jetty with the little boy clinging to her.

Marco knelt on the jetty and held out his hand to lift Nicky out of the water. 'Stand there and don't move,' he ordered.

Adrenalin was still surging through his blood and his voice was harsher than he'd intended. *Dio*. He had almost lost Nicky a year ago. Watching the little boy fall into the lake just now had made him sick with terror that he might lose the only person who mattered to him for good. Guilt stabbed him as his son's big brown eyes filled with tears.

'Don't you dare tell him off.'

Leah glared up at Marco. She was treading water, and the gauzy material of her dress billowed around her, reminding him of a waterlily. He offered her his hand, and when she grabbed it he hauled her onto the jetty. Her hair had come loose and she raked her fingers through the waist-length curls.

'It wasn't Nicky's fault that he fell in. You shouldn't have allowed him to be unsupervised by the lake.'

'I *didn't* allow it,' Marco gritted. 'I believed Nicky was safely in bed. And he has been told many times that the lake is out of bounds unless he is with an adult.'

'Most children are fascinated by water.'

Marco felt Leah stiffen when he lifted his hand to her shoulder. Her skin felt like satin and his eyes were drawn to the pale slopes of her breasts that were rising and falling jerkily. He wondered if she was breathing hard simply after the exertion of swimming, but his instincts told him that she was as aware of him as he was of her.

'I was removing a leech from your shoulder,' he explained.

Her eyes widened. 'There are leeches in this lake? Ugh! Are there any more on me?'

'I can't see any.' Her soaking wet dress clung to her body and she looked like a beautiful water nymph.

'I can feel something,' she yelped, frantically pushing her fingers inside the top of her dress and pulling out a handful of weed. 'Oh, it's slimy…but at least it's not a leech.'

Nicky made a muffled noise that might almost have been a laugh. Marco froze. He had never heard his son laugh.

Leah crouched down beside the little boy. 'I think it would be a good idea for you to have some swimming lessons. But until you *can* swim will you promise not to go near the lake unless a grown-up is with you?'

Nicky nodded.

'He doesn't speak much,' Marco told Leah gruffly.

'I know.' She remained crouching beside Nicky and kept her gaze on his face. 'It's okay,' she said softly. 'I'm your friend. We've had lots of fun together while your *papà* has been away, haven't we?'

'Yes.'

Nicky's response was quiet but clear. Marco was surprised that his son had even spoken. Usually the little boy was withdrawn and silent with strangers, but Leah seemed to have established some kind of a rapport with Nicky in a way no one else had been able to.

She stood up and gave Marco a withering look that irritated him. 'I've spent quite a bit of time with Nicky while you were away. Your girlfriend often says she feels unwell, so I offered to look after him. I'm used to young children.' A small frown furrowed her brow. 'James had gone off to play golf every day. I didn't realise he was so keen on the game... But Nicky and I kept each other company.'

'Stacey is *not* my girlfriend. She is my son's nanny.'

Marco had heard the disapproval in Leah's voice and it increased his sense of guilt. She made him feel like a terrible parent, but he was already painfully aware of his failings. He did not know how to bond with his son, and he envied Leah because she had evidently won Nicky's trust.

He felt a punch in his chest when Nicky moved closer to her and gave one of his shy smiles.

Marco acknowledged that although he had come to hate his ex-wife, Karin *had* been his son's mother. Not a very good mother, from what he'd heard, but Nicky must miss her. The little boy needed someone in his life he could form a bond with. Marco had hoped that person would be him, but so far his attempts to build a relationship with the little boy had been unsuccessful.

He noticed that Nicky was shivering. Although it was a warm evening the lake would have been cold. Marco slipped off his jacket, intending to wrap it around his son, but Nicky shied away from him, so he thrust the jacket at Leah, who draped it around the little boy.

'Nicky shows many of the classic signs of post-traumatic stress. I know he lost his mother a year ago,' she said softly, 'have you sought any kind of help for him? It's much better to deal with psychological issues quickly, rather than hope the problem will simply go away.'

'I hardly think *you* are qualified to comment on my son's psychological state or offer advice about his upbringing,' Marco grated. He had a vague idea that Leah worked in an art gallery and it was there that she'd met his half-brother.

He felt defensive, because in truth he did not know how to help Nicky. The doctor at the hospital in Mexico, where Nicky had been treated after the accident, and the psychotherapist he'd found in Italy had both advised that Nicky needed time to process everything that had happened. But it had been a year and he was still suffering.

'As a matter of fact I have a degree in special educational needs and a post-graduate qualification in early years primary education. I teach children in the three-to-seven age group who have special needs.'

Leah's tone was frosty, but then she turned back to Nicky and smiled warmly at him.

'Let's get you back to the house and into the bath. Do you want your daddy to carry you or would you like to hold my hand?'

Nicky's eyes darted to Marco but he slipped his hand into Leah's. The rejection felt like another punch to Marco's chest and he shoved his hands into his pockets, avoiding Leah's gaze as they walked back along the jetty.

He'd tried everything he could think of to try to win his little boy's trust. But Nicky had been just a baby when Karin had disappeared with him. When Marco had finally been reunited with his son a year ago Nicky hadn't remembered his father.

Wet chiffon flapped around Leah's legs as she walked back across the lawn. Some of the party guests had come outside to see what was happening and she felt self-conscious as she climbed the steps up to the terrace and caught sight of her bedraggled reflection in the windows of the orangery.

She looked around for James but couldn't see him. When she walked into the house the horrified expression on James's mother's face when she caught sight of Leah was almost comical.

'Do try not to drip on the carpets,' Olivia said in a pained voice. 'Your dress must be ruined.'

'I'm sure it will be fine after a wash. Anyway, I'd rather have a ruined dress than for Nicky to have drowned,' Leah said pointedly.

She had expected Olivia to comfort her grandson after his ordeal of falling in the lake. Poor child. His grandmother seemed uninterested in him and his father was utterly heartless. She frowned as she remembered how Marco had snapped at the little boy.

Leah glanced over to where Marco was now talking to his son's very attractive nanny. Stacey was practically falling out of her low-cut dress. It was obvious that Marco had chosen the nanny for her physical attributes rather than her ability to care for a child, Leah though disgustedly.

He turned his head in her direction and she quickly averted her eyes from his hard stare. Nicky was led away by the housekeeper, a cheerful Cornishwoman named Derwa, and Stacey and Marco continued their conversation for a few minutes before the nanny walked off.

Leah was desperate to go upstairs and change out of her wet dress. From the way that it was sticking to her body she knew it was very obvious that she wasn't wearing a bra, she realised, glancing down and seeing the outline of her nipples jutting beneath the wet silk.

Then she saw Marco walking towards her, and her feet seemed to be welded to the floor. He looked breathtaking in a black dinner suit and her stomach swooped when she noticed the shadow of dark chest hair beneath his white silk shirt.

It was unfair that he was so gorgeous, and very wrong for her to find him so attractive when she was about to marry his brother. Ashamed of her traitorous thoughts, and dismayed by her fierce awareness of Marco, she could not bring herself to meet his gaze when he halted in front of her.

'I apologise if my face repulses you,' he said in a grim voice.

Her eyes flew to his face and she shook her head when he ran his hand over the scar on his cheek. 'It doesn't repulse me.'

'Then why are you so reluctant to look at me?'

'I'm not.'

'Prove it. Look at me, Leah.'

His voice was like warm honey sliding over her. Surely she hadn't heard a hint of self-doubt in his tone? Marco De Valle was the most self-assured man she had ever met.

Leah huffed out a breath. 'You must know that with or without your scar you are very good-looking.'

Something flickered in his eyes. 'And you, *bella*, look as beautiful in your soaking wet dress as you did before your impromptu swim in the lake. Which leads me to say what I should have already said, and that is thank you for rescuing my son. If it hadn't been for your quick response Nicky could have drowned.'

'You would have saved him. I just happened to be closer to the lake when he fell in.'

Did that breathless voice belong to her? Hearing Marco say she was beautiful had clearly affected her vocal cords.

He smiled, and the tight band around Leah's lungs contracted even more. His scar made his smile a little lopsided, but no less sexy.

'And now I must go and run Nicky a bath,' he murmured.

'I thought the nanny had gone to do that.'

Marco's face hardened. 'I gave Stacey the option of terminating her contract voluntarily or being fired. She decided to leave Nancarrow Hall immediately. My son's welfare is paramount,' he insisted as Leah's eyes widened. 'I regret that circumstances meant I had to rely on an agency to appoint a temporary nanny for him instead of vetting someone properly myself. And, by the way, I feel the need to tell you he has regular consultations with a child psychologist who is trying to help him.'

'Don't blame yourself for Nicky's problems,' Leah said softly. 'Your wife's death must have been devastating. You need—'

'You have no idea what I need.'

Marco cut her off, his voice as cold as the arctic, and Leah told herself she must have imagined that his inflexible mouth had ever curved into the briefest of smiles.

She couldn't explain why tears welled in her eyes as he strode away. Maybe it was the haunted look on Marco's face at the mention of his wife—as if he hurt deep in his bones, in his soul.

Leah understood the pain of loss. Not so much for her father, whom she remembered only vaguely, but because his death had been the beginning of her mother's self-destruction. And then there had been Sammy, her sweet, funny little half-brother, with his cherubic smile. She had adored him for the few precious years of his life.

She pictured the other little boy with big brown eyes, who reminded her of Sammy. Marco's son.

In her job, Leah had met many children who'd suffered emotional trauma following bereavement or the loss of a close family member. She knew from experience that Nicky was desperate for reassurance after losing his mother, and that the best person to give him the love and support he needed was his father.

But Nicky seemed wary of Marco, and it wasn't hard to understand why. Marco was an iceman. Leah grimaced as she remembered how he had been so cold towards Nicky when he'd pulled him out of the lake, instead of cuddling him and showing him the affection that the little boy clearly craved.

She wished she could help Nicky, but there was no time. Tomorrow evening she and her new husband would be on a plane, flying to the Seychelles for their honeymoon at a luxury spa hotel.

Thinking of James, she went in search of him and found him playing billiards in the games room. His face was flushed, and she guessed he'd had too much to drink.

'Whass happened to *you*?' he slurred when he saw her.

'Your nephew fell in the lake and I jumped in and pulled him out.'

'I hope the lord of the manor was impressed that you saved his kid.'

James picked up his glass and swallowed its contents. Leah wrinkled her nose at the smell of whisky and felt a familiar cramp of tension in the pit of her stomach—a throwback to her childhood, when her mum had started drinking heavily.

'Why did you call Marco the lord of the manor?'

'He owns this place.'

James laughed at Leah's obvious surprise.

'Marco inherited Nancarrow Hall from his father—my mother's first husband. Vincenzo De Valle bought the house when they married, but he died suddenly, leaving all his assets—including the coffee business in Italy and the Nancarrow estate here in Cornwall—to Marco, his son and heir. Marco was just a kid, so the house was held in trust and run by my mother. A couple of years later she married my father and I was born. Nancarrow Hall was our home. When Marco was eighteen he became the legal owner. He allows us to continue to live here, but he never lets me forget that I am reliant on his charity. Marco is the one with the money,' James said sulkily. 'You're marrying the wrong brother, sweetheart.'

'You are the man I want to marry,' Leah assured him softly.

She felt relieved that she had an explanation for why James had seemed so moody since they had come to Cornwall. He resented his older half-brother. Perhaps he also suspected that she found Marco attractive, she thought, with a mixture of guilt and shame. No other man unsettled her the way Marco De Valle did. Luckily he lived in Italy and she was unlikely to meet him very often, she reassured herself.

'Tomorrow is the start of our life together,' she murmured as she moved closer to James and pressed herself up against him. She tilted her face and parted her lips for his kiss, but he turned away from her.

'You're all wet,' he muttered. 'You had better go and get changed.'

'Why don't you come upstairs and help me take my dress off?' she asked. Tomorrow she would become James's wife, and it suddenly seemed ridiculous that he had never seen her naked.

He looked awkward. 'There'll be plenty of time for that sort of thing when we're on our honeymoon.'

Leah felt a flicker of foreboding at James's lack of enthusiasm. Asking him to come to her bedroom and undress her had been a big step in their relationship for her, and she was confused that he had rejected her. In less than twenty-four hours they would make a vow to honour each other with their bodies, but James seemed reluctant even to kiss her.

She looked over at the bar in the games room, where James's best man Philip had lined up several bottles of spirits.

'I want to have a few drinks on my last night of being single,' James told her.

It was only natural that he wanted to celebrate his last night as a bachelor. He wasn't having second thoughts about the wedding and neither was she,

Leah told herself firmly. Marriage was all about compromise.

She smiled at him. 'Don't get too drunk. I'll see you in the church tomorrow.'

Her bedroom was in the newest wing of the house. Derwa had explained to her that the extension had been added in the eighteen-hundreds, but the original house, where the family's bedrooms were, dated back to the fourteenth century.

Leah headed straight into the en suite bathroom, peeled off her sodden dress and dropped it into the bath. It wouldn't be the end of the world if the dress was ruined, although she wished she hadn't spent so much money on it.

Amy had persuaded her to buy the striking apricot-coloured dress instead of the navy blue evening gown which, in Leah's opinion, would have been far more suitable. Her red hair meant that she tended to play safe with colours, and the apricot cocktail dress was strapless and showed off a daring amount of her cleavage—a far cry from her usual style. Leah was not daring, and she preferred clothes that allowed her to blend into the background.

She stepped into the shower cubicle, and as she shampooed her hair to wash away the smell of lake water she couldn't help feeling unsettled by James's response—or lack of it.

When they had started dating she had been grieving for her grandmother, who had died a few months earlier, and she hadn't felt ready for a sexual relationship. The truth about why she was still a virgin in her mid-twenties was rather more complicated than that, though, Leah acknowledged with a sigh. She'd dated a few guys at university, but when they had wanted to take things further than a kiss at the end of the evening she'd always broken up with them. It wasn't that she disliked the idea of sex, but finding someone she trusted enough to want to share that level of intimacy with was another matter. To her, passion suggested a loss of control.

In her mind, she heard her mother's voice. *'One day you'll know how it feels to fall wildly and crazily in love.'* But Leah had seen the way her mother's affairs had inevitably ended after just a few weeks or months, and the tears and drinking binges that had followed.

Leah did not want 'wild and crazy' in a relationship. She wanted steadiness and reliability and gentle affection. She'd been grateful that James hadn't tried to rush things. He had been sweet and patient, and it had been his suggestion to wait until their wedding night to consummate their relationship.

Perhaps that was the problem, she brooded. James seemed so on edge since they had been at Nancarrow Hall because he was frustrated, but he was clearly determined to honour his promise to wait until they were married before they had sex.

After her shower, Leah wrapped herself in a robe and returned to the bedroom. The rehearsal dinner would be finished by now, and there was no point in her going back downstairs. She left her hair to dry naturally rather than make any inexpert attempts to blow-dry it. Anyway, the hairdresser who had been booked to come to the Hall early in the morning planned to style her unruly curls in an elegant 'up-do'

She flicked through the TV channels but gave up when nothing caught her attention. There was a bottle of wine chilling in an ice bucket in her room. She sent Amy a text, asking if she wanted to join her for a pre-wedding drink.

Moments later, her bridesmaid texted back.

I'm with Philip in the boathouse!

She followed it with a thumbs-up emoji.

Amy had set her sights on the best man, and it was no surprise that the couple had got together. Leah envied her friend's uncomplicated attitude to relationships.

'Have you really never had casual sex?' Amy had once asked her.

Leah hadn't admitted that she'd never had *any* kind of sex.

She sighed. If Amy was with Philip it seemed likely that James had finished drinking. Perhaps he had gone to bed. Common sense suggested it would be a good idea for her to get an early night before the wedding too.

She opened a drawer and took out one of the oversized T-shirts she usually slept in. Folded next to it was the daring black chemise that Amy had persuaded her to buy for her honeymoon. On impulse, Leah slipped the chemise over her head and stared at her reflection in the mirror.

It was amazing how a wisp of silk and lace made her look different. Sexier. Her red hair was the bane of her life and she kept it tied up most of the time. But now it tumbled around her shoulders and spilled over her breasts, which were inadequately covered by the flimsy nightwear. The silky chemise felt sensual against her skin and she noticed that her dark areolae were visible through the sheer lace cups.

She imagined olive-tanned hands cupping her breasts, strong fingers sliding the straps of the chemise down her arms, baring her to the gaze of grey eyes, which would be gleaming as he bent his head and closed his mouth around one taut nipple…

No! *Wrong man. Wrong fantasy.*

Leah pressed her hands against her hot face, but she could not banish the erotic images of Marco touching her body. She had *wanted* him to kiss her in the church, she admitted shamefully. It was as though he had awoken a desire that had lain dormant for all her adult life—until now.

CHAPTER THREE

WAS SHE HER mother's daughter after all?

Despair swept through Leah. As an adult, she looked at her mum's choices of unsuitable lovers—men who had been selfish and sometimes brutal—and wondered how Tori could have been so weak, following her heart and letting her actions be dictated by her sexual desires.

Leah had always been proud of her own common sense, but now she understood what her mum had meant about falling crazily. Not in love but in lust. Want, need.

She had never felt those things until she'd met Marco.

But she was about to marry James.

Why had she thought that marrying for security and safety would guarantee happiness?

Leah buried her face in her hands as she realised she had been fooling herself. Passion and desire were important elements in a loving relationship, but she didn't even know if she and James were sexually compatible. She bit her lip as she remembered how he had spurned her tentative advance earlier, when she'd invited him to her room.

She *must* make love with James tonight!

The realisation struck Leah like a thunderbolt. She could not make a solemn promise to spend the rest of her life with him while the huge question of whether they desired each other remained unanswered.

She was not by nature an impulsive person, but she didn't wait to consider more carefully if she was doing the right thing and tore out of her room before her nerve failed.

James's room was in the old part of the house. Leah had only been there once before, when she'd gone to look for him after he'd been late meeting her to go and play tennis. The butler had escorted her along a maze of passageways, but now she'd have to try to find the way on her own.

The lamps along the landings were dimmed at night, and twice she took a wrong turn. But she remembered that there had been a large Grecian urn on a table next to the door of James's room.

Leah halted in the corridor and wiped her damp palms down her chemise. Tension cramped in the pit of her stomach and she took a deep breath and tried to relax. This was the right thing to do, she assured herself. Once she had made love with James it would put an end to her doubts about their relationship and she was sure that her fascination with Marco would disappear.

Leah stepped into the room and closed the door behind her, shutting off the chink of light from the passageway. The darkness was impenetrable, but as her eyes adjusted she could make out a four-poster bed. Her heart was beating painfully hard. She hadn't expected to feel nervous about having sex for the first time—surely it was way overdue, she thought wryly. But what other reason could there be for her reluctance to put into practice what she had come here to do? Why did every thud of her heart urge her to retreat back to her room? James *was* the right man for her, she told herself.

Maybe if she told herself enough times she would be convinced.

She stiffened when she heard the mattress creak. 'Are you awake?' she whispered.

The muffled response could have been a snore or a sleepy grunt of surprise. Leah resolutely ignored the clamour of doubts in her head and climbed onto the bed.

'I know you must be surprised that I've come to your room, but I want you to make love to me.'

She crawled along the mattress and almost lost her nerve when her hands skimmed over hard thighs. She felt the outline of powerful muscles through the sheet. Moving higher, she discovered hip bones and a taut abdomen.

She leaned forward, bracing herself with her hands on either side of his head, so that her breasts were pressed against his chest. His face was shadowed, but Leah was glad of the concealing darkness as she bent her head and sought his mouth. She brushed her lips across his and instantly it felt as though a bolt of electricity had zapped right down to her toes.

Relief swept through her. There had been no need for her to doubt that sexual chemistry existed between them. Every nerve-ending in her body tingled with anticipation.

'Kiss me, *please*.' She whispered the words into his mouth.

He hesitated for a fraction of a second before he obeyed.

Leah's heart slammed against her ribs when he moved his lips over hers—gently at first, and then with an increasing passion that made her tremble with needs she did not fully understand, which evoked an ache low in her pelvis.

He was heat and fire and she melted, stretching her body out on top of his. Strong arms curved around her, trapping her against his powerful physique as he pushed his tongue inside her mouth. Leah had never experienced such an intensity of passion before. Her heart sang and her spirit soared as she matched him kiss for kiss, and he made a rough sound that was muffled against her lips.

The sheet was a barrier between their bodies. She gave a moan of frustration that turned into a sigh of pleasure when he pushed his hand between them and spread his fingers possessively over one breast. Her nipple peaked and thrust against the lacy barrier of her chemise.

Everything was going to be all right. The flood of

warmth between Leah's legs was proof that she was ready to give herself completely and exclusively to him.

'I want to have sex with you,' she said breathlessly. 'I don't want to be a virgin for a moment longer.'

'A virgin? *Madre di Dio!*'

Before she knew what was happening Leah found herself lifted by strong hands and dumped unceremoniously on the mattress. The bedside lamp was switched on and she blinked in the sudden bright light.

'You!' Incomprehension turned to shock, horror and finally toe-curling mortification as she stared at Marco. 'Where's J-James?' she stammered. 'Why are you sleeping in his room?'

'This is my bedroom. James's room is directly above mine on the third floor.' Marco leaned back against the headboard and narrowed his eyes on Leah's hot face.

She silently cursed her fair skin. But far worse than her tendency to blush easily were her navigational skills.

'Oh, God!'

This had to be the most humiliating moment of her life.

'Seriously? You're a virgin?'

Leah felt the heat on her face spread down her neck and across the upper slopes of her breasts so very revealed by the skimpy chemise. 'It's none of your business,' she choked.

'It would have been very much my business if you had seduced me into having sex with you.'

The hint of laughter in Marco's voice was unex-

pected. She hadn't known that he was capable of
laughter, so grim and forbidding as he was. But the
fact that *she* was the source of his amusement made
Leah want to slap the mocking grin off his face.

'I wasn't trying to seduce *you*. I thought you were
James. It was dark and I couldn't see you,' she said
tautly when Marco raised one eyebrow. 'I went to the
wrong room by mistake.' She jerked at the strap of her
chemise which had slipped off her shoulder, pulling
it back into place. 'I feel a complete idiot. Why didn't
you stop me?'

'*Cara*, when I am woken by a woman begging me
to have sex with her I rarely refuse.'

'It happens to you a lot, does it?' she snapped.

For some reason, the thought of Marco taking his
pleasure with other women who were far more beautiful and sexually experienced than her evoked a sensation like a sharp knife shoved between Leah's ribs.

He wouldn't take his pleasure selfishly; he would
give the utmost pleasure to his lovers. She had no idea
how she was so certain of that, but her pulse accelerated when she looked at him and found he was studying her with eyes that gleamed bright and sharp, as if
he could see inside her head.

'I enjoy sex as much as every other red-blooded
male,' he said, folding his arms behind his head and
drawing Leah's attention to the bunched muscles in
his shoulders. Her gaze dropped to his broad chest,
covered with crisp, dark hair that arrowed down his
flat abdomen and disappeared beneath the sheet. It oc-

curred to her that he might be naked, and her breath became trapped in her lungs.

'You must have guessed that I'd come to the wrong room and I believed you were James,' she muttered.

'No, *cara,* I assumed it was *me* you wanted to have sex with.'

If her face burned any hotter she would combust. 'Why would I want to sleep with you when I'm about to marry your brother?'

'A good question,' Marco murmured with a hint of laughter in his voice again. 'Perhaps James doesn't excite you? That must be the case if you haven't allowed him to take you to bed yet.'

'It was a mutual agreement to wait until we were married,' Leah said stiffly.

'If you were *my* fiancée you would not want to wait—and I sure as hell wouldn't be able to keep my hands off you.'

The lazy amusement in Marco's tone had disappeared. He sat up straighter, so that the sheet slipped down dangerously low, and stared at her with an intensity that made her feel dizzy and weak—and, worse, tempted her to lean forward and cover his hard, sexy mouth with hers.

She knew the beauty of his kiss now. A little shiver ran through her as she remembered how his lips had moved over hers with bold assurance and devastating sensuality.

She should go. *Now.* Get out of his room and be thankful that he had stopped her before it was too late.

But the common sense that she prided herself for possessing seemed to be taking a holiday.

She tilted her chin belligerently. 'I did not beg you for sex.'

'Yes, you did. And what's more you *knew* it was me you were kissing.'

Marco gave her a sardonic look as she shook her head wildly, so that her curls flew like red sparks around her shoulders.

'You might be a virgin, but you must have kissed James. You know what his mouth feels like beneath yours. You know his taste. And now you know mine,' he said harshly.

His words hovered in the air, challenging her to deny them. Leah had thought he was a terrible man and now she knew just how lethal he was. If she lived to be one hundred she knew she would still see his face in her dreams. The perfection of his sculpted features, the darkness of his unshaved jaw, the tragedy of the scar that for some inexplicable reason made her want to weep.

'I believed I was kissing James.'

It was the truth, she insisted to herself. But her conscience reminded her that the kisses she'd shared with James had never blown her mind or made her tremble with desire the way she'd trembled when Marco had clamped her against his body and she'd felt the hard ridge of his arousal through the thin sheet.

It wasn't fair to compare the two men, she thought desperately. If she and James had become lovers before he had brought her to Nancarrow Hall she would not have developed a silly schoolgirl crush on his half-brother.

She waited for Marco to say something, but his silence filled the room and the oxygen was sucked from her lungs when he pinned her with his brooding stare. His eyes roamed over her, and to her horror she felt her nipples harden so that they pushed against the sheer lace cups of her chemise.

Galvanised by the molten gleam in his gaze, Leah scrambled across the mattress. 'I'm going to find James.'

Her conscience would not allow her to marry him tomorrow after the way she had responded to Marco tonight. Leah knew it was only fair that she admitted to James her reservations about their relationship.

'I made a genuine mistake when I came to your room,' she told Marco. 'I'd be grateful if you would forget that anything happened.'

'Nothing of any consequence *did* happen. Trust me, if it had you would be begging to remain in my bed for the rest of the night,' he said lazily.

His arrogance took Leah's breath away, but before she could slide off the bed his hand shot out and he caught hold of her arm. This time when he spoke his voice was low and unexpectedly fierce.

'Take my advice and go back to your room. Don't visit James tonight.'

'I've already told you that I don't want your advice.' She jerked free from his grasp and ran over to the door.

'Leah.'

His husky accent turned her name into a caress. She

paused with her hand on the doorknob and turned to face him, knowing it was a mistake—another mistake.

Marco shoved a hand through his thick hair. He was still sprawled on the bed, propped up on one elbow—indolent and far too sexy for his own good. He was a disaster waiting to happen, but he wouldn't be *her* disaster.

Leah thought again of all the men her mother had given her heart to, only to have her romantic dreams shattered time and time again. 'I'm not listening to you.' She clung to the doorknob as though it was a lifeline.

'You will be making a mistake if you marry James. Come here and let me prove it to you.'

For one terrible, shameful second she was tempted. 'You have no right to say such things,' she said huskily. 'Where is your loyalty to your brother?'

'Perhaps you should discuss *loyalty* with James.'

'What do you mean?'

Marco swore and raked his fingers through his hair again, as if he needed an outlet for his restless energy. 'It is not for me to comment on your relationship with your fiancé,' he said gruffly.

'Then don't.' Leah tore her gaze from his and opened the door. 'I'm going to see James and nothing you say will stop me.'

A flight of stairs at the end of the corridor led to the third floor. Leah tore along the hallway and saw a Grecian urn on a table—a replica of the one outside Marco's room on the landing below. Light filtered beneath the door of James's bedroom and she guessed that he was still awake.

She knocked, but she was too agitated to wait for a response and flung the door open. 'We need to talk... *Oh!*'

Her words died on her lips and she stared in stunned disbelief at Davina the wedding planner, in bed with James.

'Leah! What the blazes are you doing here?' James demanded, while his companion dragged the sheet over her naked breasts.

'I'd like to ask Davina the same question,' Leah said, frozen in the doorway, too shocked to be able to think clearly. Her legs felt wobbly and she clutched the doorframe for support. 'I don't understand.'

But the situation was humiliatingly clear. James had rejected her because he'd planned to spend the night with Davina.

'I thought you loved me,' she whispered, feeling more of a fool than she had ever felt in her life.

James blew out a breath. 'The truth is that I was never in love with you, Leah.'

Marco shoved his hair off his brow with a hand that remarkably—for a man who never, *ever* allowed himself to be affected by a woman—was not entirely steady. He should have stopped Leah. But not from crawling all over him while she pleaded with him to make love to her.

His mouth dried at the memory of her nubile body stretched out on top of him.

He had been half asleep, and for a heart-stopping moment he'd thought that the erotic fantasy he'd been having about Leah had come true. She'd looked incredible, in a sexy black negligee that had framed her voluptuous breasts. His blood had heated as he'd anticipated stripping her so that he could trace his lips over her silken skin. But then she had gone and ruined it when she'd said that she was a virgin.

Dio. How was that even *possible*? She was the most responsive woman he'd ever put his mouth on—and there had been many, Marco acknowledged. He'd had his fair share of lovers before and after his marriage—but not during it. He happened to believe that marriage was a serious commitment, which was why he intended never to do it again. One cheating, lying ex-wife was enough.

A message flashed on his phone, advising him that the movement sensor alarm on the third floor had been activated. He thought of Leah, on her way to offer herself to James. Muttering a curse, Marco slid out of bed and pulled on his robe, wincing as the towelling brushed against his still uncomfortably hard erection.

He should have stopped her from running out of his room. All it would have taken was him tugging her back down onto the bed and kissing her until she made those little moans in the back of her throat that he'd found such a turn-on.

He could still taste her…honey and vanilla on his tongue. She'd insisted that she'd believed she was kissing James, but was that true?

He strode up the stairs and along the third floor

landing, halting next to one of the ugly Grecian urns that his mother collected. Leah was standing in the open doorway to James's room, her hands gripping the frame. Marco sensed that if she let go her legs would buckle beneath her.

'I thought we were friends, Davina,' she said in a choked voice.

Marco felt no surprise that the wedding planner was in his brother's room. At the wedding rehearsal he had tried to suggest to Leah that she should postpone marriage until she'd had a chance to know James better, and this was why.

There was a sweetness about Leah that made Marco wish he could have saved her from the pain of disillusionment. But she would get over it with time, he thought. And if she had any sense she would learn that love was a lie put about by poets and dreamers.

He was about to return to his room, but Leah was speaking again, and Marco succumbed to curiosity and withdrew into an alcove in the passageway.

'James, if you have never loved me, why did you ask me to marry you?'

'Your inheritance,' James muttered. 'I owe a lot of money to some people who are likely to get nasty if I don't repay them soon. I borrowed heavily, to invest in a business deal that promised amazing returns, but then the goldmine in Africa flooded and I lost my investment. I can't ask my parents for help because my father advised me against the deal.'

Marco rolled his eyes. It wasn't the first time James had sunk money into a get rich quick scheme that had failed. He'd bailed his half-brother out many times in the past and refused to do so again.

'How on earth did you find out about my inheritance?'

Leah sounded shocked, and it struck Marco as odd that she had tried to keep something like that a secret from her future husband.

'Amy mentioned it that night she introduced us at her party. She was drunk, and she told me that you had been left millions of pounds by a relative, but couldn't claim the money until you were married. To be honest, you seemed like the perfect answer to my problems.'

'I don't think I ever told Amy the exact amount of my inheritance, but it isn't millions. How disappointed you would have been after you had gone to all the trouble of pretending to be in love with me.' Leah's voice trembled. 'All you wanted was my money. That's despicable.'

'Don't act so righteous.' James sounded sulky and defensive. 'You're not in love with me, either. Amy said you were desperate to get your hands on your inheritance. That's why you were so eager to marry me, isn't it? We were both willing to use each other.'

Leah did not deny James's accusation.

Marco frowned. He'd been feeling sympathy for her—even a degree of guilt. If he had given his half-brother the loan he'd asked for James would not have tried to trick Leah into marriage. But now it sounded as though Leah had a strong incentive of her own, he thought as he made his way back to his bedroom.

He paused outside the nursery and opened the door,

entering the room quietly. Nicky preferred to sleep with a nightlight, and the soft glow from the lamp danced across his black curls. His impossibly long eyelashes fanned on his cheeks.

Marco's heart clenched. He would never forget the first time he'd held his son in his arms. His marriage had already been strained, but he had been instantly smitten with his baby boy and had vowed to do everything he could to create a happy family life for his son.

When Karin had disappeared with Nicky the pain Marco had felt was indescribable. It had been more than three years before he'd seen his son again, in Mexico, where Karin had been living with her lover, a low-life crook. Who knew what kind of life Nicky had led for those crucial years of his early development? The little boy had never spoken about what had happened to him, and Marco felt powerless to connect with this son who regarded him as a stranger.

He leaned over to tuck the bedcovers around Nicky, curious when he saw a piece of paper sticking out from beneath his pillow. Marco carefully slid the paper out and stared at the childish drawing of a person with long, curly hair drawn with an orange crayon. There was no doubt that the picture was meant to be of Leah, and the smaller black-haired figure holding her hand was Nicky's attempt to draw himself.

Marco turned the paper over, wondering if his son had drawn him, but the other side was blank.

As he slipped the drawing back under Nicky's pillow and returned to his own room he recalled the trusting expression on the little boy's face when he'd clutched Leah's hand after she had fished him out of the lake. It was nearly midnight, but he felt too wired to sleep.

Pulling back the curtains, he glanced up at the moon, suspended like a silver disc in the inky sky. He was puzzled when he saw a figure by the gate which led from the garden onto Bodmin Moor. She was silhouetted in the moonlight, but even from a distance Marco recognised Leah. He watched her walk a little way onto the moor and then hesitate where the path forked before turning in the direction of Hawk's Tor.

What the hell was she doing out on the moors at night?

Leah was not his responsibility, he reminded himself, but he knew how easy it was to become lost in such a remote place. He swore as he pulled on jeans and a sweater then strode out of his room.

As a boy, Marco had spent many hours walking on the moors after his father's death, but his absence from the house had mostly gone unnoticed. His mother had been widowed for just a year before she'd married Gordon Fletcher. Ten months later she'd given birth to James and Marco had been sent away to school. Olivia had paid little attention to her eldest son when he'd come home for the holidays.

Marco had always felt an outsider at Nancarrow Hall, and as soon as he'd become an adult he'd settled in Capri and made Villa Rosa, the house owned by three generations of the De Valle family before, his permanent home.

But he knew from those lonely hikes across the moors that the weather could change quickly, even in summer. He exited the house and garden, following the route he'd seen Leah take. A breeze had blown up, sending clouds scudding across the sky so that every now and then the moonlight was obliterated.

Earlier, Marco had called one of his security personnel, and within the hour had received confirmation of Leah's academic and professional qualifications. Her experience in teaching children with special needs, and the bond she seemed to have formed with Nicky, meant that Leah might be the one person who could help his little boy.

CHAPTER FOUR

THIS COULDN'T BE the shortcut to the village. Leah peered through the darkness, hoping to see a light in a cottage window or some other sign of civilisation. But there was nothing apart from the outline of a stunted tree which had been bent and twisted by the wind that whipped across the moors.

She'd fled Nancarrow Hall because she hadn't been able to bear to stay after she'd been so humiliated. She never wanted to see James again after his betrayal. But although she was bitterly angry with him, she was also furious with herself too, for making such an error of judgement. She had seen in James what she had wanted to see, Leah acknowledged. Her longing for security had made her ignore her doubts about their relationship.

As for Marco…

A shudder of embarrassment ran through her when she remembered her inexpert attempt to seduce him, believing he was James. It was all immaterial now, she thought grimly. She had accidentally gone to Marco's room, but it had been no accident that the wedding planner had been in bed with James.

A sob rose in her throat, but she brushed her tears away. Crying wouldn't help a situation that had gone from bad to disastrous.

After she had discovered James's duplicity she'd rushed back to her bedroom. Her phone had been ringing, and Gloria, her mum's neighbour in London, had explained that Tori had collapsed in the street and been taken by ambulance to hospital.

'I think your mum had been drinking again,' Gloria had said gently. 'She was upset and kept asking where you were.'

'Thanks for letting me know,' Leah had said.

She'd felt a mixture of shame at Tori's behaviour and guilt that she hadn't been around to help her. She'd known she needed to return to London immediately, but couldn't ask James to drive her. So she'd left a note for Amy and left.

But she must have taken the wrong path to the village and now she was lost on the moors. Leah looked back over her shoulder and felt a ripple of fear when she could not see the Hall. She had walked further than she'd realised. The moon had disappeared and the darkness was thick around her.

That eerie noise was just the wind, she told herself. She froze when she heard another indistinguishable sound that seemed to be getting closer. Someone or something was following her. An animal, perhaps? But what sort of animal?

Her heart was thudding as she felt in her jacket

pocket for her phone. The *no signal* icon flashed at the top of the screen. She switched on the phone's torch and gasped when she saw a huge figure coming towards her. This night from hell was rapidly turning into a nightmare! Leah's emotions were already in a fragile state and her imagination took over from her common sense.

'What do you want? Get away from me!' She started to run but stumbled on the uneven ground. The harsh, panting noise was her own breaths, she realised. 'Leave me alone!'

'Leah!'

The voice was shockingly familiar. She held up her phone so that the torchlight flickered over Marco's chiselled features and revealed the scar carved into his cheek.

'Oh, it's you.' She released a shaky breath as her fear evaporated. But her heartrate accelerated when he came closer and she caught the drift of his spicy cologne. 'I thought…' She shook her head. 'Your housekeeper told me there are legends about evil spirits and other strange phenomena who roam the moors.'

'Did you think I was the Beast of Bodmin?' Marco asked drily, running his hand over his scar.

'I don't know what I thought.' Leah couldn't hold back a sob. Reaction to the night's events was hitting her hard and she buried her face in her hands.

'What are you doing, wandering around the moors in the dark?'

'I was trying to get to the village, and from there to the station at Bodmin.'

'At midnight?'

'I couldn't remain at the house and see the pitying expressions on everyone's faces tomorrow. Did you know that James and Davina are lovers? I suppose you did as you warned me not to go to James's room,' she said dully. 'Apparently they started an affair in London soon after I hired Davina to organise the wedding. For the past week James has been meeting Davina in secret at a hotel in Padstow, instead of playing golf, as he told me. And tonight I found them in bed together.'

Her voice cracked.

'The wedding is off, in case you were wondering. Davina has just found out she is pregnant. That's why she looked so upset at the wedding rehearsal. James says he is going to stand by her.'

Marco tugged her hands away from her face and stared at her, his eyes glittering hard and bright. 'You have been crying.' He sounded surprised.

'What did you expect?'

Leah had not been able to hold back her tears. She was hurt that James had lied and her pride was dented. In addition, with the wedding called off she would not be able to claim her inheritance, and now worrying about her mum made her feel as if she was balanced on an emotional tightrope.

'I feel such a fool for believing that James was in love with me. I thought he was different to other men I'd dated, and he didn't put pressure on me to go to bed with him.'

'*Cara*, if he didn't want sex with you it was because his interests lay elsewhere,' Marco said bluntly.

'Sex is not the most important part of a relationship,' she argued. 'There's love and trust.' She gave another sob. 'I trusted James.'

'But you didn't desire him or you would have wanted to sleep with him.'

Leah bit her lip. Marco's assessment was too close to the truth. She *hadn't* felt a burning desire to have sex with James—or any other man. Well, one other man, she thought shamefully, remembering how her body had ached for fulfilment when she'd stretched out on top of Marco and felt the hard proof of his arousal.

On a subconscious level she *had* realised that he wasn't James, she acknowledged. Marco was the man of her fantasies—but she wasn't about to admit to the effect he had on her.

He towered above her, darkly beautiful in black jeans and a matching fine wool sweater. He was inherently dangerous to her peace of mind and he evoked a longing in her that no other man had ever done.

For too long Leah had supressed her sensuality, but now it blazed, needy and desperate. She swayed towards him and her tongue darted across her lips, issuing an unconscious invitation.

He stared at her mouth and there was something primitive about the stark hunger in his gaze. She wished he would haul her against his muscular body and carry her away into the darkness. Out here on the ancient moors they were simply a man and a woman drawn together by a desire as old as mankind.

She could feel the urgent beat of her pulse, the sharp pull of her nipples and the flood of molten warmth between her legs. She heard the unevenness of his breath and felt the tension that emanated from him. A shaft of moonlight revealed his skin stretched tightly over his razor-edged cheekbones.

He slowly lowered his head and she held her breath, waiting, wanting…

Abruptly he stepped back from her and shoved a hand through his hair. 'I'll show you the way to the village.'

He took her holdall from her nerveless fingers and walked off in the opposite direction to the one she had taken when she'd left the house.

Reality kicked in, bringing memories of the phone call she had received from her mum's neighbour. 'I need to catch the train to London,' she said as she hurried after Marco.

'You're too late. The last one has already left. But you can stay at the pub tonight.'

She struggled to keep pace with his long strides and was out of breath by the time they reached the village. There were no lights on at the Sailor's Arms. The sign hanging on the post creaked. 'Of course the pub is closed now,' Leah muttered, feeling sick at the thought of returning to Nancarrow Hall and having to face James tomorrow.

Marco slipped his phone into his jeans pocket. 'I sent a message to the landlord asking him to prepare a room for you.'

'Won't he mind that it's so late?'

'I own the pub,' Marco said drily. 'The whole village belongs to the Nancarrow estate.'

He led Leah round to the back door of the pub and ushered her into the tiny bar.

'This is Bill.' He introduced the man who had walked through from another room.

The landlord took Leah's holdall. 'I'll carry your bag upstairs, Miss Ashbourne. Come up when you're ready and I'll show you to your room.'

Marco moved towards the door. 'Try to get some sleep,' he advised. 'I'll come back in the morning. I have a proposition that I want to discuss with you.'

Leah's imagination went into overdrive. Those moments on the moors when Marco had looked at her with hunger in his eyes, as though he wanted to devour her, burned bright in her memory.

'What sort of proposition?'

He laughed softly and his grey eyes gleamed with amusement and something else…an intentness that made Leah supremely conscious of her femininity.

'Not the sexual kind,' he drawled. 'I'm afraid you will have to play out those fantasies with someone else. I don't take wide-eyed virgins to bed.'

She ground her teeth as Marco's grin widened. 'You really are the most arrogant beast,' she snapped.

Her insides squirmed. How could he know that she'd had erotic fantasies about him? Was her fascination with him so obvious? Leah wished that the trapdoor in the pub floor would open so that she could leap into the black void below.

Marco lifted a hand to his face and traced the line of his scar. 'It's true. A beast *is* what I am.'

There was no laughter in his voice now, just a grimness that hurt Leah although she could not explain why.

He caught hold of her chin and tilted her face up to his. 'You would do well to remember that, Beauty.'

She stared into his eyes—not cold as an arctic sky, but gleaming like molten silver, glinting with promise and a wicked intent that made her tremble.

'Tell me the truth,' he said softly. 'Did you know that you had come to my bedroom instead of James's?'

Leah bit her lip. She was innately truthful, but she did not dare admit to Marco that *he* was the man she had been thinking about when she'd left her room.

'I was confused,' she muttered.

He gave a harsh laugh. 'You proved when you kissed me that you have passion and fire. How could you have contemplated a passionless marriage?'

'I didn't know that I could feel such strong desire,' she whispered, 'until…'

Marco's eyes glittered. 'Until?' he prompted.

'Until I came to your room and…and kissed you.' The damning words left her lips on a sigh.

Her heart leapt when his head swooped down and he claimed her mouth with devastating authority. She was impatient for his kiss and pressed herself against him, tipping her head back, softening her lips and parting them beneath his.

He tasted divine, and the spicy tang of his aftershave mixed with the almost imperceptible scent of male pheromones was more intoxicating than any drug. Flames swept through her body, setting every nerve-ending alight. Marco was demolishing her barriers with terrifying ease, and she felt unmoored, scared of the firestorm he had unleashed inside her and yet compelled to burn in the conflagration.

He muttered something in Italian against her lips as he slid his hand along her jaw, commanding her with a flick of his tongue to open her mouth and allow him access. But then—shockingly—he wrenched his mouth from hers and captured her wrists, pulling her arms down from where she had wound them around his neck.

Leah stared at him in confusion which quickly turned to embarrassment with the realisation that the panting breaths she could hear were *hers*, not his. He set her away from him and she knew she must have imagined there was a look of regret in his grey gaze.

'Sweet dreams, *bella*,' he said, in that mocking way of his that made her hate him and hate herself more. Because she could not resist him and he knew it.

Surprisingly, Leah slept soundly. The kindly landlord had brought a mug of hot milk to her room the night before, explaining that he'd added a tot of Irish malt to help her sleep. It must have worked.

When she opened her eyes, sunlight was poking in through the gap in the curtains. It looked as though it would be a perfect day for a wedding.

She felt a pang of regret for the dream that she now realised would have quickly turned sour. James hadn't loved her, and in her heart she knew she had not been in love with him. But she had imagined herself to be in love with him precisely because he did *not* arouse strong emotions in her, and she had felt in control.

Her reaction to Marco was far more worrying. She certainly wasn't in love with him. She didn't even *like* him. But when he'd found her on the moors she had wanted to surrender to him.

Dear heaven!

Where had *that* thought come from?

Leah covered her burning face with her hands. What had happened to her determination to listen to her head, not her heart—or in this case her hormones? What she felt for Marco was lust—wild and unrestrained lust. It had taken over her body with its insistent demands, and she was suddenly terribly afraid that she was like her mum after all.

Her phone rang, and she gave a small sigh when she saw Tori's name on the screen.

'Mum, how *are* you? Are you still at the hospital?'

'The doctor in A&E said I could be discharged once I'd sobered up. Gloria came and drove me home.' Tori was crying so hard that it was difficult for Leah to understand her. 'Oh, Leah, I've made such a mess of my life. Last night I just wanted to drink until I forgot everything.'

'What did you want to forget?' Leah asked gently.

'The money…' came the almost incoherent reply.

'What money?'

'The money I took from work.'

Foreboding slithered down Leah's spine. 'Mum! Stop crying and tell me what you've done.'

'It started two Christmases ago,' Tori said dully.

'Remember you saw that lovely coat in the shop on the high street? You said it was too expensive, but I wanted to buy it for you. You're a good girl, Leah, and you deserved a nice Christmas present. But I couldn't afford it.'

Leah loved the grey wool coat with its exorbitant price tag. 'You told me you'd bought that coat in a pre-Christmas sale.'

'I paid full price for it. I wanted to see you happy, darling. I know I've been a useless mother to you. It was easy to borrow a few hundred pounds from the company. Chris Hodge is a good builder, but he knows nothing about finance and accounts. I made up a couple of fake invoices and paid the money into my own bank account.'

'God! Mum, that's fraud.'

'I planned to pay back what I'd taken. But then I fell behind with the rent and there were other bills. When Sammy's grave was vandalised I felt like I'd lost my precious little boy all over again.' Tori wept harder. 'I took a couple of thousand pounds from the company to pay for a new headstone. Every time I made up a false invoice I promised myself that I'd put back all the money I'd taken. But last week the auditors did a cash-flow report and discovered what I'd been doing.'

Leah slid out of bed and crossed to the window to pull back the curtains. Scattered clouds raced across the blue sky, sending shadows dancing over the moors. In the distance a bird of prey hovered perfectly still before it swooped towards the ground. She wished she was a bird, soaring free in the sky.

'What will happen now that your theft has come to light?'

'Chris has been very good about it. That's the worst of it—knowing that I've betrayed our friendship. He's given me to the end of the month to repay all the money, and he's going to allow me to resign rather than be sacked.' Tori's voice trembled. 'But if I don't put the money back he will call the police. Leah, I could go to prison. I know I've done wrong, but I can't bear the idea of being locked up. I wish I wasn't here any more. I want to be with Sammy.'

'*Don't* talk like that, Mum.' Leah pinched the bridge of her nose and forced back her own tears. 'Everything will be okay.'

She had some savings, and she might be able to get a bank loan—although she would need to find a job quickly. Her teaching contract at a special educational needs school in London had finished at the end of the summer term, and she'd intended to wait until after the wedding before looking for a new placement.

'How much money do you owe?'

'It's about...well, just over thirty thousand pounds.'

'*Thirty* thousand?' Leah felt sick. There was no way she could raise that amount—certainly not at short notice.

'Leah, I'm sorry...'

Tori sounded like a small child, and in many ways their roles *had* been reversed, Leah thought. She'd always had to be the responsible one and take care of her mother. That was why Grandma Grace had left Tori, her only daughter, out of her will and bequeathed her money to her granddaughter.

'I'll think of something, Mum. Try not to worry,' Leah murmured before she ended the call.

She had no idea what she was going to do, though, and frustration surged through her when she remembered her grandmother's last will and testament.

I give to my only granddaughter, Leah Rose Ashbourne, the sum of five hundred thousand pounds.

Half a million pounds was more than enough to save Tori from a possible prison sentence and cover the cost of private treatment for her alcohol addiction. Leah had also hoped to buy a flat for her mum, so that she could make a fresh start. But the stipulation in Grandma Grace's will was a major stumbling block and there seemed no way around it.

The money is only to be made available on the date of my granddaughter's marriage.

Of course her grandmother had been entitled to dispose of her assets as she'd seen fit. And Grandma Grace had held the quaint belief that every woman needed a good and supportive husband.

Perhaps it was because her grandparents had enjoyed a happy marriage for nearly sixty years before her grandad had died, followed two years later by her gran, Leah mused. Tears filled her eyes. She missed her grandparents. When she was a child, she'd loved going to stay with them. But those visits had been rare events because Tori hadn't got on with her parents and they had disapproved of her unconventional lifestyle.

Thinking of her mum pulled Leah's mind back to the present. Standing around and moping would not solve anything, she told herself firmly. It sounded like the plot of a Victorian novel—but she needed to find herself a husband.

Marco checked the ground-floor reception rooms but there was no sign of Nicky. He raked his fingers through his hair, feeling guilty that he'd been on his phone dealing with an urgent issue at De Valle Caffè instead of having breakfast with his son.

'He refused to eat anything,' the housekeeper had reported. 'I only went into the pantry for a minute, and when I came back to the kitchen he'd gone. The back door is locked, so he can't have gone outside.'

Derwa had rested her hands on her hips.

'Mr Marco, what shall I do with the wedding food that has already been prepared? It seems a terrible shame to throw it away.'

'What about offering it to the local care home? I'm sure the elderly residents there would enjoy smoked salmon blinis.'

As Marco strode up the stairs he told himself that Nicky could not have disappeared altogether. But the boy was not in the playroom, or his bedroom. He continued his search, feeling ever more frantic as he walked from the old part of the house into the newer wing, where the guest bedrooms were located.

It was early in the morning and no one else was up yet. He felt no sympathy when he thought of James having to explain to the guests the reason why the wedding had been cancelled.

The door to Leah's room was open and he gave a sigh of relief when he saw Nicky sitting on the bed.

'Hey, there you are.' Marco crouched down so that he was at eye level with his son. 'We're going back to Capri today.' He frowned as Nicky shook his head. 'Don't you want to go home?' The little boy said nothing, and Marco sighed. 'Come on, it's time to go.'

'Leah.'

Shock jolted through Marco. He felt as though his heart was being squeezed in a vice when he saw the little boy's unhappy face. Nicky had not cried since the accident. It was as if his emotions had been frozen since he had lost his mother. But now he had asked for Leah.

Marco automatically ran his hand over the scar on his cheek. He hated Karin for depriving him of his son for the first three years of his life, but he wished he had been able to save her for the little boy's sake.

He gently wiped Nicky's tears away. 'Would you like Leah to come to Capri with us?'

There was nothing he would not do for his son, Marco thought when Nicky nodded. Somehow he must persuade Leah to accompany them to Italy.

When he'd walked back across the moors to Nancarrow Hall after he had kissed her the previous night, he'd realised that he had to have her. And with her wedding plans in ruins, he had seen no reason to deny himself. A brief affair with her, on his terms, would suit him.

He visited London regularly for work, and he had planned to lease an apartment in the capital and establish her there as his mistress. Undoubtedly the chemistry between them would burn out after a few weeks, or months at most, and he would move on. Their white-hot attraction couldn't last. In his experience it never did.

But now the situation had changed, and he wanted Leah to help his son. That meant he must ignore his inconvenient hunger for her.

Denial was meant to be good for the soul, Marco reminded himself a short while later, after he had left Nicky in the kitchen with the housekeeper, making pancakes.

He drove the short distance to the village. His pilot was preparing his jet, ready for their flight to Naples later on, and Marco was determined that Leah would be on the plane with them.

'Miss Ashbourne is still in her room,' the landlord told him when he entered the pub. 'She asked for some coffee but didn't want breakfast.'

The Sailor's Arms dated back to the thirteenth century and had once been the meeting place of a local smuggling gang. Marco ducked his head to avoid the low ceiling beams as he climbed the stairs. He knocked on the door at the end of a narrow corridor and Leah opened it almost immediately. She was even paler than usual, and her eyes were the slate-green of a stormy sea. Tears clung to her copper-coloured eyelashes.

'I was just about to leave,' she said flatly, hooking her fingers under the strap of the holdall hanging from her shoulder. 'There's a train to London at nine-forty.'

Marco braced his hands on either side of the door frame. 'Had you forgotten that there is something I want to discuss with you?'

'I hadn't forgotten, but I'm not interested in your proposition.'

'That's not the impression you gave me last night, *bella*.'

He was fascinated by the flush of rose-pink that stained her face. Before she could stop him he stepped across the threshold, so that she had no option but to back into the room. Her obvious distress puzzled him. When he'd overheard the conversation between Leah and James last night it had not occurred to Marco that she might be emotionally invested in his half-brother. He was surprised by how much he disliked the idea.

'How do you know you're not interested when I haven't explained what I want from you yet?'

Without giving her time to speak, he pressed on.

'I am offering you a job as my son's private teacher. When I tried sending Nicky to school he became deeply upset, and I was advised to keep him at home until he had recovered from the distress of losing his mother. But I'm concerned that he will fall behind in his education. I want you to stay at my home in Capri so that you can work with Nicky every day. I know you have experience of teaching traumatised children and I know you have formed a bond with my son.'

Leah shook her head. 'I can't help Nicky. I'm sorry.'

Every vestige of colour had drained from her face and she looked tense and unhappy.

Marco was frustrated by her flat refusal. 'But Nicky likes and trusts you. I've checked your qualifications and your employment record and I believe you are the best person to help him.' He exhaled heavily when she continued to shake her head. 'I will pay you generously.'

Instead of replying she turned away from him and walked across the room to stare out of the window. Marco let his eyes roam over her, admiring the way her jeans moulded her pert derriere. She had restrained her hair in a braid again, and he longed to untie it and sink his hands into her riotous curls while he covered her mouth with his.

He swore beneath his breath as he felt his body's predictable response to his erotic thoughts. Somehow he would have to ignore this desire for Leah.

'There is nothing I will not do for my son,' he said deeply. 'Name your price.'

She swung round to face him and hugged her arms around her slender body. Marco had the odd sense that she was trying to stop herself from falling apart.

'My price is marriage. Marry me before the end of the month and I will do my best to help Nicky.'

CHAPTER FIVE

'I'M FLATTERED,' MARCO said drily. 'Have you fallen in love with me? Is that why you are so eager to be my wife?'

'Of course I'm not in love with you.' Leah had been aiming for the same mocking tone Marco had used but her voice emerged annoyingly husky.

His brows rose. 'Then I assume your urgency to get me to the altar is so that you can claim your inheritance?'

She stared at him. 'Does the whole world know about my inheritance?'

'When you left my room last night you set off a movement sensor linked to the burglar alarm system. I followed you so that I could reset the sensor and I overheard you talking to James.'

'So you are aware of the stipulation in my grandmother's will that I must be married before I can access the money she bequeathed to me?'

Leah couldn't believe what she had done. She must have lost her mind to demand that Marco marry her in return for her helping his little boy. But she was desperate to keep her mum out of prison.

He had offered to pay her well if she went to Capri to work as Nicky's teacher, and she had briefly considered accepting the job and asking him for an advance on her salary. But she needed thirty thousand pounds immediately, so that Tori could return the money she had stolen.

It was unlikely Marco would be sympathetic if she revealed that her mother was a thief and had a drink problem. Leah remembered the shame she had felt as a teenager, when a teacher at school had asked if her mum was an alcoholic and gently suggested involving social services. Out of loyalty she had refused to betray Tori, and she would not do so to Marco now.

She forced herself to meet his enigmatic gaze. He was her only hope of claiming her inheritance. She did not have prospective husbands queuing outside her front door, she thought wryly. Besides, she had become fond of his son. She felt sorry for Nicky and wanted to help him.

'What I am suggesting is a temporary marriage while I work with Nicky to try and build his confidence.'

Her heart missed a beat as Marco strode towards her. He dominated the small bedroom, but it was not just his size and impressive physique that made Leah feel that the walls were closing in around her.

His charcoal-grey suit was undoubtedly bespoke. The elegant jacket was undone to reveal a navy blue silk shirt stretched across his broad chest. He wasn't wearing a tie, and the top few buttons of his shirt were open so that she could see a vee of olive-tanned skin and a sprinkling of black chest hair.

He halted in front of her—too close for her peace of mind. The exotic scent of his aftershave sent a coil of heat through her and she despaired of herself when she felt her nipples tingle. She crossed her arms tighter over her chest, to hide the betraying signs of her awareness of him.

'You admit the reason you want to marry me is money?'

He spoke in a lazy drawl, but his eyes were coldly contemptuous and Leah realised that he was furious.

'*My* money, not yours,' she said quickly. 'I know you are wealthy but I'm not a gold-digger. And it wouldn't be a real marriage.'

'In what way would it not be real?'

'Well, we wouldn't…sleep together.' Her voice faltered when his dark brows drew together.

'Perhaps you would like me to be neutered?'

There was no humour in his wolf-like smile. And his low, dark laugh sent a quiver through Leah. She realised then how much danger she was in. Not from Marco, but from her body's instinctive response to his potency.

'What makes you think I would agree to a sterile marriage with a virgin bride?'

She bit her lip. 'I've explained that it wouldn't be a proper marriage and I realise you will want to take a mistress.' Leah could not understand why she so disliked the idea of him sleeping with another woman.

'How very understanding of you, *cara.*'

The bite in his voice made her flinch.

'But if I decide to accept your proposition it will be on *my* terms, not yours, and I will have certain expectations. Number one being that you *will* share my bed.'

Leah hated the way her body responded to Marco's silky voice, but she could not control the spike of heat that centred deep in her pelvis as shockingly erotic images filled her mind of his naked limbs entwined with hers.

She swallowed. 'Are you saying you would force me to have sex with you?'

His jaw hardened, and there was no mistaking the furious glitter in his eyes. 'I have never forced a woman to do anything against her will. I find the idea abhorrent and frankly I'm insulted by your suggestion. I know you want me, *bella.* You proved it when you came to my room last night and crawled all over me.'

'You know I made a mistake when I came to your room,' she said hotly.

'I know you are a liar—to yourself as well as to me.'

He drew back his cuff and glanced at his watch. Leah couldn't help noticing the black hair on his wrist, that curled around the gold watchstrap. She imagined those darkly tanned hands touching her body, those long fingers dipping between her thighs and moving higher, seeking her feminine warmth…

'I gather from your silence that marriage to me has lost its appeal now you know what it will entail?' Marco said drily. His eyes narrowed on her flushed face before he swung round and walked back across the room. 'The train to London leaves in fifteen minutes. I'll give you a lift to the station.'

'What about Nicky?' Leah said sharply. 'I'm sure I can help him.'

Her heart softened when she thought of the little boy who reminded her so much of Sammy. Thankfully Nicky did not suffer from a rare degenerative disease, as her brother had, but there was a vulnerability about Marco's motherless son that tugged on Leah's emotions. All children needed a mother's love.

She sighed when she thought of her own mother. Tori hadn't been a conventional parent, but Leah had never doubted that her mum loved her.

Marco shrugged. 'I'll find another teacher for him.'

He had reached the door and started to open it.

'Wait.' She could hear her heart pounding in her ears, drowning out the voice of caution. 'I'll be a proper wife to you.'

He turned around slowly and pinned her with his searing gaze. Leah did not understand the reason for the simmering fury in his eyes.

'Clarify that statement,' he bit out.

Common sense told her that she should retract her damning words before the hole she was digging for herself got even deeper. But something stronger than reason and the sensible rules she had lived by all her life compelled her to lift her chin and meet his gaze.

'I'll have sex with you…if I have to.'

Marco closed the door and leaned back against it, crossing his arms over his formidable chest. 'How enticing,' he said sarcastically. 'You make it sound as if you will be doing me a favour, but the reverse is true. Initiating a virgin is tedious, or so I've heard. Especially if that virgin is metaphorically clutching at her pearls and feigning distaste of carnal pleasures.'

'Why, you arrogant...' Words failed Leah.

Humiliation scorched her cheeks. So Marco thought that having sex with her would be tedious? Never had she wished more fervently that she was as sexually confident and experienced as most of her friends. She was sorely tempted to tell him to go to hell. But if he walked away now she would never see him again.

It was that thought above any other that made her lift her chin and meet his hard stare. 'What do you want from me?' She felt near to tears and painfully out of her depth, but she refused to show any sign of weakness in front of him.

'Not to be a sacrificial lamb, that's for sure,' he drawled. 'You will have to try harder to persuade me that it would be a good idea to marry you.'

So he hadn't ruled out marriage. Hope flickered inside her. 'How?' she asked.

'I suggest you think of something fast. I'm growing bored.'

Once again Leah sensed that he was angry, although she still did not understand why. When he had kissed her last night, before he'd left her at the pub, she had felt sure he desired her. And now she had agreed to make their marriage real. But maybe he needed to be convinced that she would keep her word and sleep with him.

The reality of what she had done caused her nerve

to falter. Was she *really* prepared to lose her virginity to a man who held all the aces up his sleeve?

Then Leah thought of her mum crying on the phone and knew that she had no choice. If Tori was charged with theft from her employer there was every chance she would be given a custodial sentence. She was already emotionally fragile, and prison would destroy her.

'Goddamn you…'

Anger surged as hot as molten lava through Leah's veins. She'd always prided herself on being calm and level-headed, but she was *furious* at the situation she was in. She would rather walk over hot coals than marry Marco. He was everything she disliked in a man—arrogant and cocksure, certain that he was irresistible to women. She seethed at the memory of how he had called her uninteresting. It would give her great pleasure to make him eat his words.

Casting aside caution, she gripped the hem of her sweatshirt and pulled it over her head. 'There. Does that persuade you?'

'Not particularly.'

His facial muscles did not even move when he lowered his gaze to her plain white bra. To her chagrin, he yawned.

Leah had to admit that her underwear was functional, rather than decorative. But Marco's lack of even a flicker of excitement acted like a red rag to a bull, goading her to elicit a response from him.

Reaching behind her back, she unclipped her bra and tugged the straps down her arms. The bra slipped to the floor leaving her breasts bare. Her skin felt cool after the warmth of her sweatshirt. It was for *that* reason that her nipples had hardened, she told herself.

The old, sensible Leah was appalled by what she had done, but this new, fiery Leah, who she did not recognise as herself, rested her hands on her hips and tilted her chin belligerently.

Marco did not look bored now.

Leah's heart clattered against her ribcage as he stared at her naked breasts with an intentness in his gaze that sent a shiver over her skin.

'*Sei squisito.*'

His voice was deeper than Leah had ever heard it. Something moved within her—heat and flame and an ache that was so strong it hurt. She knew that *squisito* meant exquisite, and the hungry gleam in his eyes evoked a fierce need inside her.

'Untie your hair,' he growled.

His husky demand rolled through her and, although the sensible Leah despaired at her inability to disobey him, she quickly unravelled her long plait and tugged her fingers through her curls. The feel of her silky hair on her naked shoulders was deliciously sensuous. She was aware of her feminine strength and her weakness for him—only for him.

Her pulse accelerated when Marco covered the space between them in two strides. 'Are you satisfied now?' she asked him sweetly, with a bravado she hadn't known she possessed.

'If you think I will be satisfied by an incomplete striptease you have a lot to learn, *cara.*'

To her surprise, he bent down and picked up her bra and sweatshirt from the floor.

'Get dressed,' he said curtly. '*Dio*, you must want your inheritance very badly if you are willing to give away your virginity so inconsequentially. Do you want to tell me why you need the money?'

Leah shook her head. Something in Marco's rough tone made tears prick her eyes, and for a second she was tempted to confide in him. But why should she trust him? If she told him about the money her mum had taken he might decide that he did not want the daughter of a thief to teach his son—and he might refuse to marry her.

'You can relax,' he said drily, perhaps guessing that she was so tense she might snap. 'For now, all I want from you is your professional expertise and your commitment to help my son. I assume you have your passport with you?'

When she nodded, he continued.

'I had planned to take Nicky to New York in a couple of weeks, to visit my cousin and her children, but I'll bring the trip forward and we'll fly to America immediately. We can marry twenty-four hours after obtaining a marriage licence there. My lawyer will draw up a pre-nuptial agreement, which you will sign, stating that you will not be entitled to receive any financial provision from me when we divorce.'

Elation swept through Leah. He was handing her a lifeline which would save her mum from prison. But could she really marry a man who was almost a stranger and who aroused feelings in her that she did not understand?

'I've told you that I don't want your money,' she said huskily. 'Once I have a marriage certificate I will be able to claim my inheritance.'

Marco gave her a cynical look. 'The contract will also set out all the additional terms of our marriage—specifically that you will live in Capri for a year and work to the best of your ability to help my son overcome his trauma.'

'A year?' Leah could not hide her dismay. 'I was thinking of a couple of months... I really do want to help Nicky,' she said quickly, when Marco frowned, 'but I can't put my life on hold for a *year*.'

He captured her chin in his lean fingers and brought her gaze up to meet his. 'Nicky has formed an attachment to you and he needs stability. My son's welfare and happiness are all I care about. Not the games we play and not you. I strongly advise you never to forget those facts.'

Leah held his gaze before shifting away from him and touching her jaw where Marco's fingers had been. Marco looked so grim and forbidding that her heart sank.

'My God, I've made a deal with the devil,' she whispered as the enormity of what she had done sank in.

His eyes gleamed as cold and hard as polished steel. 'I told you what I am, Beauty. You should have heeded my warning. It's too late to back out now.'

He must be out of his mind! Marco tightened his hands on the steering wheel as he drove away from the pub.

He could not believe that Leah had demanded he marry her before she would help Nicky—and that he had agreed! He was incensed that she had in essence blackmailed him and then told him that she did not want a real marriage.

But he had called her bluff when he'd insisted that he would want her to be his wife in every sense. He'd expected her to back down from her marriage demand then. And when she'd primly agreed to sleep with him, making her reluctance obvious, and even worse suggested that he might *force* her to have sex, his temper had skyrocketed.

He'd wanted to teach her a lesson, but what had happened next had tested his self-control to the limit.

Marco swore as he remembered how Leah had taken off her bra to reveal pale breasts tipped with rosy nipples. She was beautiful, and he had been fiercely tempted to kiss the sweet curves of her body before tumbling her down onto the bed.

But he had reminded himself that she was out of bounds. He hoped only that Leah would bring Nicky out of his shell and help him come to terms with the loss of his mother.

Marco frowned as he thought of Karin. When the car she had been driving had crashed and burst into flames he'd had to choose between pulling his son or his ex-wife out of the wreckage first. Nicky had been his priority and Karin had died.

He could not give Nicky back his mother, but he had promised the little boy that Leah would come to Capri with them. And if accepting her marriage deal was the only way he could make his son happy he would go through with it, Marco vowed grimly.

In Central Park, two days later, Marco stood a little away from Leah and watched her rub sun lotion onto Nicky's arms. New York was in the grip of a heatwave, and the bright sunshine had encouraged the turtles in the park out of the water to bask on the rocks—much to the little boy's evident delight. He hadn't stopped smiling since they had arrived at the pond.

'Look, Nicky, there's another one.' Leah pointed to the water. 'Do you think your *papà* would like to see the turtles too?' She looked over her shoulder and beckoned to Marco.

He stiffened when he saw Nicky's smile disappear. The wary expression on the little boy's face made his heart clench. It was clear that his son preferred to be with Leah—he had hardly left her side since they had boarded the plane for their flight to America.

At least she genuinely seemed to care about Nicky, and for that reason Marco had organised the necessary paperwork and booked a wedding officiant to marry them tomorrow.

His phone rang and he answered it when he saw his PA's name on the screen. Thinking about work stopped him thinking about his failure as a father.

During his conversation he was aware of Leah glaring at him before she turned away and knelt beside Nicky. Minutes later Marco finished the call. He wished he could just stroll over to the pond and crouch down beside his son, so they could watch the turtles together. It would be the most natural thing for a father to do. But he did not know how to connect with Nicky. He envied Leah's natural affinity with the child—the way she ruffled his hair and slipped her arm around his shoulders to gently draw him away from the water's edge.

It was obvious that she was good with children—which must be important in her job as a special needs teacher. But Marco was curious. He had sensed a sadness in her sometimes when she was with Nicky. Perhaps she had hoped to have children of her own when she'd planned to marry James. He frowned as he remembered his half-brother's accusation that Leah had only wanted to marry him so that she could claim her inheritance.

Clearly the money was important to her. Why else would she have issued her outrageous marriage demand to him? Marco brooded. But he had spent a good deal of time with her since they had arrived in New York and she did not strike him as someone who was obsessed with money or impressed by it.

Her motives were of no interest to him, he reminded himself. All he cared about was the connection she had formed with his son.

Against his will, his gaze was drawn again to Leah. Her outfit today was a shapeless dress in an unbecoming beige colour. The previous day she'd worn a navy blue skirt with a hemline way below her knees and, as always, had had her hair scraped back from her face and tied in a schoolgirlish braid.

But her unexciting clothes did not disguise her natural beauty. She would look stunning in a dress that made the most of her gorgeous figure, and breathtaking without any clothes on at all.

Marco expelled a ragged breath. Usually when he was interested in a woman he slept with her, and then his fascination tended to fade quickly. Perhaps the fact that Leah was off-limits served to increase his interest. He'd never had to deny himself before, he acknowledged wryly. Money and power were aphrodisiacs to many women and the truth was that he'd become jaded.

Leah looked over at him again. 'Nicky would like to go in a rowboat. Is there somewhere to hire one?'

Marco pointed to a building across the park and the three of them walked along the path to a restaurant which offered boats for hire. Leah put a lifejacket on Nicky, and helped him into the boat, but she shook her head when Marco climbed in and held out his hand to help her aboard.

'I'll stay here and keep in the shade, under the trees. I forgot to bring a hat, and I feel as though I've had too much sun,' she said.

It was true that her nose and cheeks were pink. Marco guessed that Leah's fair skin would burn easily, but he couldn't help thinking that she had made the excuse so that he would be able to take Nicky in the boat without her.

He looked at his son. 'Okay, are you ready?'

He half expected that Nicky would refuse to go without Leah, but after hesitating for a moment he nodded.

As Marco rowed across the lake he looked around at the other families who were having fun on the water and felt an ache in his heart. Nicky had never had the support of both his parents because Karin had disappeared with him when he was only a few months old. Now his mother was dead.

An inquest had confirmed that Karin had died from the impact of the crash, before the car had caught fire. There was nothing he could have done to save her, Marco knew.

He studied Nicky's grave little face and sighed. If Leah had come in the boat Nicky would be enjoying himself. Marco was annoyed that she had forced him into a situation where he was alone with his son. He had no problem chairing a meeting of the company's directors, or negotiating a deal in a boardroom, but he was struggling to think of something to say to a five-year-old.

'Look, Nicky, there's a heron.' He pointed to the tall grey bird standing on the bank. The bird spread its wings and took off, soaring gracefully into the sky.

'Herons are big,' Nicky said in his soft voice. There was a rapt expression on his face as he watched the bird fly to the opposite side of the lake. 'How can they fly, *Papà*?'

Marco searched his mind for facts about the heron's biology. 'Well, you can see that they have very wide wings, and they use the strong muscles in their bodies to flap those wings. And their long beaks allow them to catch fish to eat.'

'There's another heron!' Nicky pointed to a white bird in the reeds.

'I think that one is an egret.'

'You know lots of things, *Papà*.'

Nicky fixed his big brown eyes on Marco and for once he did not look wary.

'We could buy a book and learn some more about herons and other birds if you like.'

His heart contracted when his son gave a tentative smile. It was the most response he'd ever had from the little boy, and it gave him hope that he would be able to start rebuilding a relationship with Nicky, with Leah's help.

But he still resented her marriage demand, and he resented even more the inconvenient desire she aroused in him. Marco was determined not to forget that marrying Leah was a business deal.

CHAPTER SIX

THE HOTEL'S PENTHOUSE suite had stunning views of
New York. Central Park looked like a green oasis amid
the iconic skyscrapers, and in the distance the Hudson
River glinted like a silver ribbon. It had been a relief
to Leah to step into the air-conditioned building and
escape the heat outside.

Nicky had been tired after their trip to the park, and
Leah had settled him in front of the TV in his bedroom
to watch cartoons for half an hour.

She returned to the lounge, where Marco was sitting on the sofa, working on his laptop. As always, the
impact of his stunning good-looks made her catch her
breath, and the coward in her wanted to retreat to her
own bedroom. But she forced herself to ignore her
awareness of him while she discussed his son.

'Nicky enjoyed going in the boat with you.'

'Good.' Marco glanced at her briefly before turning his attention back to his screen.

Leah frowned. 'But you need to try harder with
him.' She did not understand Marco's attitude. 'For

half the time we were at the park you were on your phone.'

'I am the head of a multi-billion-dollar company and I'm rarely off duty. Nicky was having a good time watching the turtles with you.'

She marched across the room and shut the lid of his laptop. 'That poor little boy has lost his mother, and you are so distant with him. Nicky acts like you're a stranger rather than his father.'

'That is because until a year ago I *was* a stranger to him.' Marco's hard features showed no expression. 'I was divorced from Nicky's mother and I did not see my son for three years.'

'Why didn't you visit him?' Leah could not hide her shock.

Something flickered on his face but disappeared before she could try to guess his thoughts.

'It was…difficult.'

His phone rang yet again. Did he sleep with it clamped to his ear? she wondered.

'I suppose you were too busy with your work schedule to have time to spare.'

Marco's eyes glinted with anger, but Leah was too angry to care. She walked across the room while he answered his phone.

She remembered how Sammy's father Jez, who had been her stepfather for a couple of years, had cleared off after her half-brother had been diagnosed with an incurable brain condition. As the disease had progressed Sammy had needed round-the-clock care, and she had helped her mother as much as possible. It had been a difficult and ultimately tragic time, and it had been after Sammy had died, that Tori had started drinking heavily.

Leah stood in front of the huge windows that overlooked the park. This hotel was reputedly the most expensive place to stay in New York, but the luxurious surroundings meant nothing to a little boy who needed love.

Nicky must have been only a baby when his parents had divorced, and he would have been too young to remember Marco. He must have felt desperately alone when his mother had died and he'd been reunited with a father he did not know, who was cold and unfeeling.

She knew it would be very easy for her to become emotionally attached to Nicky. But she must not, she reminded herself. Her marriage to Marco was to be a temporary arrangement, and thankfully there was no danger of her emotions being involved with him.

The hairs on the back of her neck prickled and she turned her head and found he was standing beside her.

'I wish you wouldn't creep up on me,' she said crossly, feeling herself blush.

The spicy scent of his aftershave assailed her senses and her breath caught in her throat as her eyes clashed with his enigmatic grey gaze.

One dark brow lifted. 'I wonder if jet-lag has made you irritable? These shadows suggest a lack of sleep,' he murmured, tracing his finger lightly over the purple smudges beneath her eyes.

Leah swallowed. He was invading her personal space, but she couldn't bring herself to move away from him. She felt the betraying tightening of her nipples and hated how her body responded to Marco's potent masculinity.

'That was my aunt on the phone. She is in New York, visiting her daughter and grandchildren, and is on her way here to the hotel to collect Nicky. They are all going to the zoo this afternoon and Nicky has been invited to sleep over with my cousin's children tonight.'

'I'll go with him if your cousin won't mind me staying at her home,' Leah offered.

'That won't be necessary. Nicky met Chiara and her family when we stayed at my aunt's house in Tuscany a couple of months ago. He likes the children, and it will be better if he is not at our wedding tomorrow. I've decided not to tell him that we are getting married—at least for now. He is too young to understand.'

Leah nodded. It made sense not to risk confusing or upsetting a little boy who had been through so much.

'But before my aunt arrives you'll need to put this on.'

Her heart missed a beat when Marco took a small box out of his pocket and opened it to reveal an exquisite ring. The stunning green centre stone was surrounded by a circle of diamonds that sparkled in the sunlight.

'The gemstone is a tourmaline,' he explained. 'My aunt is a die-hard romantic and she will think I chose the ring to complement the colour of your eyes.'

'Is this really necessary?' Leah asked, stiffening when he reached for her hand. 'I assumed that our marriage would be secret. After all, it will end once we've both had what we want from it.'

'Thanks to social media, secrets tend not to stay secret for long,' Marco said sardonically. 'I am a well-known figure in Italy and the paparazzi take a great interest in my private life. It will be better to make a public announcement of our marriage rather than have a nosy journalist expose it in the newspapers and start digging around for a scandal.' His brows rose. 'Do you have any dark secrets I should know about?'

Leah bit her lip, worried at the idea of a reporter finding out about the money her mum had stolen. 'Do *you* have secrets?' she countered.

She could not decipher the expression that flickered on Marco's face. 'I prefer not to have my personal life used as tabloid fodder. If we attempt to keep our marriage a secret people will wonder what we are hiding. Obviously Nicky does not read newspapers, so he won't find out. And I have already told my mother and James that we are getting married.'

Leah gave him a startled look. 'What did they say? I can't imagine Olivia was pleased. She made it plain that she believed I wasn't good enough for James, and I imagine she feels the same way about me marrying you.'

'My mother has never taken much interest in what I do,' Marco said drily. 'James offered his congratulations and said that he intends to marry Davina before their baby is born.'

'I see.'

Leah felt a flicker of envy for the wedding planner,

who would now have the security and family that *she* had dreamed of. But then she reminded herself that neither she nor James would have been happy if they had married.

She pulled her thoughts back to the present and watched Marco slide the ring onto her finger. It fitted perfectly, as if it was meant to be there. For no reason that made sense tears pricked Leah's eyes. Of course he had not *really* chosen the ring because the tourmaline matched her eyes. He had probably ordered any ring from the jeweller without specifying a style or gemstone.

She sighed. It had seemed a simple idea to marry him so that she could claim her inheritance, but the reality was proving to be far more complicated.

'You will need to act like an adoring fiancée in front of my aunt. She won't understand that we are marrying for convenience and it will be simpler to allow her to believe that we are in love,' he drawled, in that cynical way of his.

'I'm not that good an actress,' Leah muttered.

'Then I suggest you learn—fast. When our marriage becomes public knowledge the board members and shareholders of De Valle Caffè will be interested because I am the CEO of the company. It is another good reason why there must not be a whiff of scandal about our relationship.'

'How am I supposed to pretend that I adore you when I don't even *like* you?' Leah asked curtly.

Marco laughed. 'You gave a very good impression

of liking me when you came to my room in the middle of the night and kissed me.'

Her cheeks reddened. 'Do you *have* to remind me of a night I'd rather forget?'

'I wish I could forget it too, but I can't.'

His voice had roughened. Leah's eyes flew to his face and she felt her heart kick in her chest when she saw that his jaw was tense and his skin was drawn tightly over his sharp cheekbones.

She licked suddenly dry lips and Marco gave a low groan as his gaze focused on her mouth. He lowered his head towards her.

'What are you doing?' she whispered, mesmerised by the predatory gleam in his eyes.

'I want to kiss you, *cara*. And I think you want me to—don't you?'

'It's not a good idea...' Her protest sounded unconvincing. If only her brain would work, she might remember *why* she should ignore the tumultuous desire coursing through her body.

'It's a terrible idea,' he agreed thickly. 'But you are a madness I can't seem to control.'

His lips were so close to hers that she felt his warm breath on her skin. And Leah offered no resistance when he brushed his mouth over hers. She wanted his kiss, and she could not fight her longing any more.

She opened her mouth beneath his, and her breath left her on a soft sigh of pleasure when he ran the tip of his tongue over her lips, exploring their shape. He moved his hand to cradle the back of her head while he continued to kiss her with a sensual expertise that made her shake as starbursts of pleasure exploded inside her.

It was impossible to control the thunder of her heart. Desire swept like molten lava through her veins. With a low moan she pressed her body against his and surrendered to his sorcery. She did not have the willpower to deny him when it meant denying herself what she wanted: his lips possessing hers, his strong arms around her, drawing her against the solid expanse of his chest. She opened her mouth at the demanding flick of his tongue, and as her eyelashes swept down he filled her senses.

Marco's skin felt warm to her touch as she ran her fingertips over his muscular arms with their fine covering of silky black hair. She dipped her tongue into his mouth and he tasted like heaven. The evocative smell of his cologne filled her lungs and she heard his ragged breaths echoing hers as she was lost to the hungry demands of his kiss…

'You look suitably ravished, *cara*. My aunt will certainly believe we can't keep our hands off each other.'

Marco forced himself to speak in a casual tone to hide how shaken he was by his reaction to Leah. *Dio*, it had been a mistake to kiss her, but he'd been unable to stop himself.

He felt a stab of remorse when she gave him a dazed look. Her pupils were dilated and ringed with irises of dark green—the exact colour of the tourmaline in the ring. He silently cursed his crazy impulse the previous day, when he'd left Leah with Nicky at the hotel for an hour to shop for an engagement ring even though it would have been simpler to phone a jeweller and order a standard diamond solitaire.

A knock on the door brought him to his senses and he raked his hand through his hair as he walked out to the hallway and opened the door of the penthouse.

His aunt was tiny in stature and comfortably plump. Her hair had turned white overnight when his uncle Federico had died, and this visual sign of the grief that Marco had shared still gave him a pang.

She greeted him effusively and chatted in voluble Italian while he ushered her into the lounge.

'Tia Benedetta, this is Leah,' Marco said when his aunt finally paused to take a breath. 'My fiancée and soon-to-be wife.'

Benedetta was stunned into silence for thirty seconds before she started to offer her congratulations in Italian.

'Leah is English,' Marco interrupted his aunt.

'Please forgive me. I should have guessed from your fair colouring that you are not Italian,' Benedetta said, speaking in English.

Leah smiled. 'Actually, I learned to speak Italian as a child when I lived in Italy and I'm fairly fluent.'

That was news to Marco. What other secrets did Leah have? he wondered.

He slid his arm around her waist and gave her a warning squeeze when he felt her stiffen. 'Are you going to show Tia Benedetta your ring, *tesoro*?' he said softly.

'Of course, *darling*,' she replied, in a saccharine-sweet voice that caused his lips to twitch.

The first time he had met Leah at Nancarrow Hall he'd thought she was docile and, in truth, rather boring. He should have realised that her red hair was an indication of a hot temper.

He was conscious of the firm swell of her breast pressed against the side of his chest, and he was more fascinated than he should be by the jerky motion of the pulse beating at the base of her neck. Her body fitted against his perfectly, but he tried to ignore his awareness of that as she held out her left hand to show off the glittering ring on her finger.

Benedetta threw her hands in the air and a tear ran down her lined face. 'I am crying with joy, Marco. You deserve to be happy after your sadness when Karin—'

Marco frowned.

'Your engagement is wonderful news,' his aunt said hurriedly. 'What does Nicolo think?'

'We're not going to tell him just yet. It will be better to wait until he feels more settled.'

Benedetta nodded. 'You must all come and visit me soon. I have a farmhouse in Tuscany,' she told Leah. 'Marco brought Nicolo to stay recently and he loved feeding the chickens. Where in Italy did you live?'

'In Tuscany, as a matter of fact. In a place called Calana.'

'Ah, I know it. I believe that Calana is a medieval town which was saved from developers by a group of artists who formed a commune. Are your parents artists?'

'My father died when I was very young. My mother was a painter, but she stopped painting after...' an odd expression flickered across Leah's face '...after we moved back to England.'

Marco wondered what she had been about to say. He was curious to know more about Leah's past.

But just then Nicky ran into the lounge and gave one of his quick smiles when he saw Benedetta. While the older woman made a fuss of the little boy, Marco went to pack him an overnight bag.

'Are you going to give your *papà* a hug?' Benedetta asked Nicky when they were ready to leave.

Marco wanted to scoop his son into his arms and press his face against his dark curls. He ached to hold Nicky close, but he was afraid of rushing things. There had been a breakthrough while they were in the rowboat, but there was still a long way to go before the little boy accepted him.

He forced a brisk laugh as he opened the door. 'Nicky is too grown up for that kind of thing. Have a good time at the zoo, *piccolo*.'

He watched his aunt and his son step into the lift. The doors closed and Nicky's face, dominated by those huge brown eyes, disappeared. Marco felt a hollow sensation in his chest. What if something happened to Nicky and he never came back?

He had a flashback to the agony he'd felt when Karin had disappeared with his baby son. His shock and anger had given way to raw pain as time had passed, and he'd been very aware that he was missing the important milestones of Nicky's life: his first steps, his first tooth, his first words.

Why was he letting Nicky out of his sight now?

Marco tried to control his fear. He was strongly tempted to take the other lift down to the ground floor, grab hold of his son and never let him go. But Nicky had been excited about the trip to the zoo and he would be disappointed if he wasn't allowed to go.

Marco wondered if Karin had made him out to be a monster to his son, and that was why Nicky was wary of him.

Rage at his ex-wife stirred rancid and bitter in the pit of his stomach. But still, despite what Karin had done, he felt guilt that he had been unable to save her.

'I can't *believe* you just told your aunt that Nicky is too grown up for you to hug him,' Leah muttered when she followed Marco into the sitting room in the penthouse. 'He's *five,* for goodness' sake.'

'I know my son's age,' Marco said curtly. 'I was only two years older than him when I went to boarding school.'

She stared at him. 'Your parents sent you away to school when you were *seven?*'

Perhaps having to be independent when he was so young explained why Marco seemed so self-contained.

'My father had died suddenly of an undiagnosed heart condition. When my mother married her second husband and James was born she was busy with her new family. It was easier for everyone if I was away at school most of the time.'

Leah pictured Marco, not much older than Nicky, being sent away from home while his mother doted on a new baby.

'I was two when my dad died and I don't really remember him,' she said softly. 'But you were old enough to have had a relationship with your father. You must have missed him.'

He shrugged. 'I used to pretend that he was on a business trip. My father travelled a lot for work, and I told myself that he would come back the next week, the next month…'

Something in his voice told Leah that he had never stopped waiting for his father to come home. She felt sympathetic that he had lost his dad at such a young age, but she was also puzzled.

'I don't understand why you made no effort to see Nicky after you and your wife split up. You must have realised from your own childhood experiences how important it was for him to have regular contact with his father.'

Marco walked over to the bar and poured himself a drink. 'My ex-wife moved to Mexico with Nicky after the divorce.'

Leah guessed from his harsh tone that he wanted her to drop the conversation, but she persisted. 'Is Mexico where the accident happened and your wife died? I intend to encourage Nicky to talk about what he remembers, and it would be helpful if you could tell me what happened.'

For a moment she thought Marco wasn't going to answer. He took a long sip of his drink and walked over to the window, standing facing away from her so that she had a view of his austere profile.

'Karin took Nicky out in her car. She lost control and the car came off the road. It must have rolled over several times,' he said tautly. 'When I arrived a few minutes after the accident I could smell petrol. I managed to pull Nicky out of the wreckage, but the car exploded while Karin was trapped inside. Mercifully she was almost certainly already dead before it happened.'

He ran his finger over the scar on his cheek.

'I was hit by a shard of glass when the windscreen shattered in the explosion. The cut went down to the bone. If it had been an inch higher I would have lost my eye.'

'My God! No wonder Nicky was traumatised,' Leah said, shaken by what Marco had told her.

'He was hospitalised with concussion, but thankfully he was otherwise physically unhurt.'

She frowned. 'So you were there in Mexico when the accident happened? I thought you didn't have any contact with Nicky?'

'It was his birthday, and Karin had allowed me to visit.' Marco swung round and scowled at Leah. 'Nicky was semi-conscious when I pulled him out of the car. I doubt he remembers anything about the accident. I see no point in you dragging up the past with him. He needs to move forward and your job is to build his self-confidence.'

He swallowed the rest of his drink and slammed

his glass down on the table before he strode out of the lounge. Moments later Leah heard the thud of his bedroom door being closed with barely restrained force.

CHAPTER SEVEN

MARCO HAD GIVEN Leah some insight into the terrible events of his ex-wife's death, although she sensed that he had not told her everything. Knowing Nicky had lived abroad with his mother had also given her a better understanding of why he did not have a close relationship with his son.

Perhaps he resented the change of lifestyle that being the single parent of a young child entailed?

She dismissed the idea. Marco must love Nicky. He had agreed to marry her so that she could help the little boy.

She wondered whether it had been him or his wife who had wanted a divorce. Maybe he'd still had feelings for Karin and was struggling to come to terms with her death.

She heard his phone ring and saw that he'd left it on the coffee table. The ringtone stopped, but seconds later it started again. It was probably a work-related call, she guessed. De Valle Caffè was a global business, and as CEO Marco was obviously heavily involved in running the company.

But she wondered if he used his work commitments as a form of escape from emotions he did not want to face in the same way that her mum masked her pain with alcohol. When she had first met Marco she'd thought he was cold and unfeeling, but now she was sure that wasn't true. He cared for Nicky, but he seemed to find it difficult to show his feelings.

His phone was still ringing.

The call must be important.

Leah's heart lurched at the sudden thought that it might be Benedetta, trying to contact Marco because something had happened to Nicky.

Grabbing the phone, she sped down the hallway and knocked on his door. He did not respond, and she opened the door and stepped into the room just as he strolled out of the en suite bathroom. A towel was draped low on his hips and droplets of water clung to his chest hair. He'd obviously just taken a shower.

His brows rose as Leah stared at him. 'You seem to be making a habit of entering my bedroom without an invitation,' he murmured.

She couldn't drag her gaze from Marco's almost naked body. Heat swept through her, spreading from her pink cheeks over her breasts and down to the molten place between her legs. His rampant masculinity made her feel weak as she moved her gaze over his broad chest, following the arrowing of dark hair that disappeared beneath the towel.

As he walked towards her she noticed the powerful thigh muscles that she'd felt beneath her when she'd stretched out on top of him on that fated night at

Nancarrow Hall. Her blush deepened as she recalled vividly the hardness of him pressing against her stomach...

Belatedly, she remembered his phone in her hand, which had now gone silent. 'Someone was ringing you,' she mumbled, holding the phone out to him. 'I thought the call might be urgent.'

'Thanks.' He glanced at the screen before dropping the phone onto the bed. 'Was there anything else?'

The gleam in his eyes told Leah that he had noticed her gaze flick towards the big bed.

'I...um... I've decided to go out for a while.'

'Shopping?'

She shook her head. 'I thought I'd do some sightseeing as I've never been to New York before. I hate shopping,' she added with feeling.

'It wasn't a suggestion,' Marco said drily. 'We are going shopping. You need a new wardrobe. When we go to Capri there will be numerous social functions which you will attend with me as my wife. You'll need suitable clothes.'

She was irritated by his superior tone. 'What's wrong with my clothes?' Her dress was smart and unfussy and, more importantly, it didn't attract attention.

'You need to ask when you are wearing a beige *sack*?'

'It's a tunic dress and the colour is ecru...or maybe taupe.'

'I don't care what it's called. It's coming off.' Marco grinned when she gasped. 'Not right now—although I won't object if you want to take it off.' He moved his hands to the edge of the towel around his waist.

'What are you doing?' she squeaked.

'I'm about to get dressed.'

His husky laughter followed her as she fled from his room.

'I'll be done in a couple of minutes. Wait for me.'

No way! Leah thought as she grabbed her handbag on her way out of the penthouse.

The lift whisked her down to the foyer, but when she emerged from the hotel and blinked in the bright sunlight a man appeared at her side.

'Please come this way, Miss Ashbourne. My name is Aaron and I work for Mr De Valle.'

A sleek, black car had pulled up next to the kerb and the man opened the rear door.

'If you'd like to get into the car Marco will join you in a couple of minutes.'

Leah found herself politely but firmly bundled onto the passenger seat, and when she looked to the front of the car the chauffeur smiled at her in the rearview mirror.

'Good afternoon, ma'am.'

Escape was impossible, she realised when she saw Aaron standing on the pavement in front of the car door. She wouldn't be able to open the door on the other side of the car because of the steady stream of traffic on the road.

Minutes later Aaron held the door open and Marco slid in beside her.

'Do you always get your own way?' she snapped.

'Always, *cara*.'

Amusement gleamed in his grey eyes as she shifted further along the seat away from him.

'Is Aaron your PA?'

'He's one of my security team.'

'You have a *bodyguard*?'

Leah supposed she shouldn't feel shocked. Out of curiosity she had checked Marco's profile on the internet. There was very little information about his private life, but she'd discovered that he was one of the wealthiest men in Europe. He had only been a boy when he'd inherited his father's coffee empire, and the company had been run by another member of the De Valle family until Marco had turned twenty-one and became executive chairman.

He had been a very young man when he'd had so much responsibility thrust upon him, and from what he'd told her of his childhood it was not surprising that he'd learned to be self-reliant from an early age. Perhaps that was another reason why he kept an emotional distance from his son.

Leah sighed as her eyes were drawn involuntarily back to Marco. He'd swapped the jeans and black polo he'd worn to the park for a light grey suit and white silk shirt. She noticed that his hair was still damp from his shower.

She noticed way too much about him, she thought ruefully, tearing her gaze from the sexy black stubble on his jaw.

'We're on Fifth Avenue,' he told her as the car crawled along in the queue of traffic. 'Over there is the Empire State Building. But there won't be time for you to do much sightseeing as we'll be flying to Italy straight after our wedding.'

Her heart missed at beat at the prospect of marrying him and her doubts must have shown on her face.

'Are you having second thoughts?'

Too many to count! But she wasn't going to admit it to him.

'I haven't changed my mind,' she told him firmly.

He put his hand inside his jacket and withdrew a document which he unfolded and handed to her. 'My lawyer has sent the marriage contract. Read through it and, if you are happy with it, sign it.'

'What if I'm not happy with it?' She bit her lip, thinking that she should ask a solicitor of her own to check the details of the contract before she signed her life away.

'Without your signature there will be no marriage,' Marco said implacably.

Grimacing, she focused her attention on the document. It stated that she would live in Capri exclusively as Marco's wife for one year and accompany him to social and business functions in support of his position as CEO of De Valle Caffè. She would fulfil the role of his son's teacher and to the best of her ability help Nicky overcome the problems caused by the trauma he had suffered. She would not be entitled to receive any money as part of a divorce settlement when the marriage ended.

'I told you I don't want your money.' She felt embarrassed that he might still suspect she was a fortune-hunter.

'So you did. But I married my first wife without a pre-nup and I have no intention of repeating the mistake,' he said sardonically as he handed Leah a pen.

She was startled by the bitterness in his voice, and glanced at his hard features before taking a deep breath and signing her name at the bottom of the document.

The car came to a halt outside an iconic designer store and the chauffeur jumped out and opened the door. Marco slid his hand beneath Leah's elbow and escorted her into the shop. She was glad of his presence beside her as she looked around at mannequins draped in beautiful clothes that she knew, even without seeing their price tags, would be way beyond her budget.

'I don't know where to start,' she muttered. 'None of these clothes will suit me. They're too colourful and too...' she searched for the right word '...noticeable.'

'You don't like to be noticed?'

She touched her hair. 'This makes me stand out too much as it is. That's why I prefer to wear neutral colours.'

'I will *not* have a wife who wears beige,' Marco growled as he steered her towards a private area at the back of the store, where an impossibly elegant woman was waiting for them.

'Mr De Valle, Miss Ashbourne, may I offer my congratulations on your engagement? My name is Julia and I am a personal stylist. It will be my pleasure to help you choose a trousseau,' the woman told Leah.

Twenty minutes later Leah had stripped down to her knickers and had wrapped a robe around her while the stylist rifled through the racks of dresses that had been brought into the changing room.

'This one will be perfect for formal evening wear.' Julia held up a full-length ruby-red velvet gown.

'I can't wear red with my hair,' Leah protested.

'You'll be surprised. Your complexion can take strong colours.'

Against her better judgement Leah stepped into the dress and the stylist ran the zip up her spine. It had narrow shoulder straps and a plunging neckline. Clever boning in the bodice pushed her breasts high without the need for a bra. The clingy velvet moulded her figure like a second skin. There were shoes to match the dress, and the four-inch stilettos had the effect of making her hips sway when she walked.

She certainly wouldn't blend into the background in this dress, she thought wryly as she studied her reflection in the mirror.

'What did I tell you?' Julia said in a satisfied voice. 'But it's not my opinion that counts.'

She pulled back a curtain and indicated for Leah to step forward into the viewing area before she allowed the curtain to fall back.

Marco was sprawled on one of the plush sofas with his long legs stretched out in front of him. He looked every inch the high-octane billionaire tycoon, with a hefty dose of sexual magnetism thrown in for good measure. As was inevitable, he was talking on his phone, but when he saw Leah he finished the call and sat up straight. The flare of heat in his eyes scorched her from across the room and a familiar weakness invaded her limbs.

She ran her hand down the velvet dress. 'I don't think...' she began uncertainly.

'*Dio*, you look incredible.'

His rough voice caused the tiny hairs on her body to stand on end, and the possessive gleam in his eyes evoked an ache of longing in the pit of her stomach.

'You should not try to hide your beauty with unflattering clothes, *cara*. In that dress you will be the centre of attention.'

That was what Leah was afraid of. At school she had been a misfit ginger-haired kid whose mum was a drunk, and she had done everything possible to avoid attracting the bullies' attention.

'Why are you shaking your head? Don't you believe me?' Marco stood up and prowled towards her like a jungle cat intent on capturing its prey. 'See, *bella*?' he murmured as he placed his hand on her shoulder and turned her to face the mirror. 'You are gorgeous.'

She stared at the mirror, but it was the naked desire stamped on his face rather than the dress that arrested her attention. She'd never had the confidence to wear clothes that flattered her figure, and she'd always downplayed her looks because she wanted to avoid attention from men. But Marco made her feel beautiful, and she noticed now how the fitted bodice of the dress made her waist seem tiny and her breasts more voluptuous.

Her eyes met his intent gaze in the mirror and heat coiled through her, centring in her feminine core.

The stylist put her head round the curtain. 'I have many more outfits for you to try on...'

But Leah had caught sight of the eye-watering figure on the price tag. Even when she converted it from US dollars to British pounds it was extortionate. Her credit card would have to take the hit. At least she would be able to pay it off when she received her inheritance.

'I'll just take this dress,' she told Julia, thinking there must be other shops in Manhattan which stocked clothes that did not cost the earth.

'My fiancée will need more than one dress,' Marco assured the stylist, who looked much happier as she disappeared back into the changing room. 'I expect you to choose daywear and evening gowns,' he told Leah. 'And I suggest you buy some new lingerie. Your bra looks as though it's a remnant from your schooldays.'

He took no notice of her angry gasp as he opened his wallet, removed a credit card and offered it to her. 'When you have finished here, the chauffeur will drive you to your appointment at a beauty salon. I have decided to follow your suggestion that I need to spend more time with Nicky, and I have called Benedetta to tell her that I'll meet them at the zoo.'

Leah shook her head, refusing to take the card. 'I won't allow you to buy me clothes. I don't want anything from you.'

'Other than my name next to yours on a marriage certificate?' he said drily.

'We both want something from our marriage,' she reminded him.

He continued to hold out the credit card, so she plucked it from his fingers and slid it into the top pocket of his jacket.

'We made a deal and that's as far as our relation-ship goes.' She ignored the dangerous gleam in Mar-co's eyes. 'You can't buy my clothes and you definitely can't buy *me*.'

A violent thunderstorm kept Leah awake for much of the night. Despite the air-conditioning in her room, the electrically charged atmosphere felt oppressive. She sat up in bed to watch the dramatic lightning that forked across a purple sky. In literature, storms were often a portent of disaster, and she could not shrug off the sense of foreboding that marrying Marco would change her fundamentally.

But of course her life was about to change. She was going to live in Capri, and she was to start structured lessons with Nicky. He was a dear little boy, and she'd found that being with him helped to ease her sadness about Sammy's death.

The prospect of her public role as Marco's wife was more daunting. Wearing designer dresses would not turn her into a sophisticated socialite, Leah thought ruefully. Besides, she had only bought a couple of new outfits, which she'd paid for herself.

She fell asleep at last and was woken by the sound of someone knocking on her bedroom door. Her heart gave an annoying flip, as it always did whenever she thought of Marco. But after she'd hastily pulled on a robe and opened the door she was greeted by a waiter who wheeled a trolley into her room. The aroma of coffee from the cafetière assailed her, and she lifted a lid to reveal a dish of freshly baked croissants.

A single white rose lay on the trolley. Leah picked it up and tears blurred her eyes as she inhaled the flower's heady fragrance. Was the rose a peace offering from Marco? She hadn't seen him since they'd argued the previous day, when he'd left her to continue shopping. If she'd been a millionaire, she would have loved to buy *all* the beautiful clothes she'd tried on. Instead she'd chosen only a few key pieces—what the personal stylist had called a 'capsule wardrobe'. The bill had been more than she had ever spent on clothes in her life and she'd winced when she'd handed over her credit card.

Her appointment at a hair and beauty salon had been more enjoyable than she'd expected. Her hair had looked amazingly glossy after the stylist had cut a few inches off the length and tamed her curls by adding some choppy layers. She'd even felt a flutter of excitement at the prospect of having dinner with Marco, but he'd sent her a text saying that after his trip to the zoo with Nicky he'd met up with a friend and did not know what time he would be back.

He hadn't returned to the penthouse by the time she'd gone to bed and she had tried not to think about the possibility that he was spending the night with a woman. She knew from the few kisses they had shared that he was an intensely passionate man. He had assured her that their marriage would be in name only, and she doubted he would remain celibate for a year.

With a faint sigh Leah placed the rose back on the trolley. As she pressed the plunger on the cafetière she noticed the *With Compliments* card.

Idiot, she berated herself. The hotel's wedding planner must have arranged for the rose to be delivered with her breakfast.

But there was nothing romantic about her wedding to Marco. It was a pragmatic arrangement and she couldn't think why she had wasted money on a dress to be married in.

She felt too on edge to manage more than a couple of bites of croissant. The marriage ceremony was to take place there in the penthouse, and the wedding officiant had been booked for ten-thirty. Leah filled the time by taking a luxurious bubble bath. After she'd dried herself, she smoothed jasmine-scented body lotion onto her skin. Her imagination ran riot as she pictured Marco kissing her neck before trailing his lips down to her breasts...

Cursing her inexplicable fascination with Marco, who was the absolute opposite of *safe*, she spun away from the mirror and forced her mind from the dangerous path it seemed intent on following.

Although her dress wasn't a bridal gown, it was made of white silk, with lace detailing on the bodice, and had narrow shoulder straps and a short skirt. With it she wore high-heeled satin shoes. She left her hair loose and clipped back the sides with diamanté slides. On impulse, she broke off the long stem of the white rose on her breakfast tray and tucked the flower into her hair.

Her heart was thumping when she walked into the lounge. The floor-to-ceiling windows ran the length of the room, to make the most of the stunning view over Manhattan, clearly visible now that the storm had passed, leaving a cloudless blue sky, but it wasn't the view that captivated Leah.

Marco must have heard her, although her footsteps had seemed to make no sound on the plush carpet. He turned away from the window and her eyes roamed over his dark suit, crisp white shirt and silver-grey tie. His thick hair was more groomed than usual, and the sexy stubble on his jaw had been trimmed. The scar running down his cheek gave him a piratical look, and the ache inside Leah expanded until the air was forced from her lungs in a ragged sigh.

'*Tesoro.*'

His voice was dark and rich like bittersweet chocolate. As he strode towards her he subjected her to a scorching appraisal; from the silky curls tumbling around her shoulders to the swell of her breasts visible above the neckline of her dress. Finally he moved his eyes down the length of her slender legs to her pretty but impractical stiletto heels.

When he looked up again Leah glimpsed an indefinable expression in his eyes, and oddly she found herself wishing this was real—that they were in love and about to promise themselves to each other for eternity.

He captured her hand and lifted it to his mouth,

brushing his lips across her fingers. 'You take my breath away,' he murmured.

A bolt of electricity shot through her fingers and up her arm, and she recalled that she had experienced the same fierce awareness of Marco when he'd stood in for James at the wedding rehearsal. Had it been only a few days ago? It felt like a lifetime since she had fled from Nancarrow Hall.

But this wasn't real, she reminded herself. The admiration in Marco's eyes, just like the tenderness in his voice, was there to convince other people that their relationship was genuine.

'Come and meet my friends,' he said, slipping his arm around her waist and drawing her forward.

Leah had only had eyes for him. But now she realised that they were not alone as a dark-haired man and an ice-cool blonde woman stood up from the sofa.

Marco introduced the couple. 'This is Paolo Bonucci and his wife Ashlyn. They live in Connecticut and flew down to New York this morning to be witnesses at our wedding.'

'It's good to meet you, Leah,' Paolo greeted her. 'I've been friends with Marco since we were at school together, but he still throws up surprises. Ashlyn and I couldn't believe it when he called us yesterday and said he was getting married again. We thought after Karin...' His voice trailed away.

Beneath his friendly tone Leah detected unease, and she saw the quick glance that passed between Paolo and his wife.

'As soon as I met Leah I knew I wanted to marry

her,' Marco said smoothly. 'Neither of us could wait—could we *cara*?'

He met her startled gaze with an urbane smile. If he ever wanted a change of career he could star on Broadway, she thought wryly. Why, he almost had *her* convinced that she was the love of his life, instead of a woman who had used his traumatised young son to emotionally blackmail him into marriage.

'We are both very happy for you.' Ashlyn smiled warmly at Leah. 'Your dress is beautiful, and I'd give anything for Titian hair like yours.'

The wedding officiant arrived, and everything felt surreal to Leah as she and Marco stood in front of her at the window, with the Manhattan skyscrapers providing a stunning backdrop.

The civil ceremony was surprisingly brief. Marco said his vows, and the slight huskiness of his voice sent a quiver through her, but she knew the words meant nothing to him and the promises he made were meaningless.

And then it was her turn. Her heart leapt into her throat when the officiant spoke to her.

'Leah, will you take Marco to be your wedded husband, to share your life with him, to love, support and comfort him whatever the future may bring?'

Leah's voice was trapped in her throat. In her mind she was a child again and she heard Grandma Grace's voice. *'Nothing good ever comes from a lie.'* But if she did not marry to claim her inheritance and replace the money her mother had stolen there was a strong chance that Tori would be sent to prison.

She could not let that happen.

Leah's eyes were drawn involuntarily to Marco's chiselled features and she took a deep breath. 'I will.'

No emotion showed in his cool stare, and when the marriage officiant announced that they were man and wife he bent his head and brushed his lips over Leah's in a perfunctory kiss.

Afterwards, they went with Paolo and Ashlyn to an exclusive restaurant for a champagne brunch. Paolo explained to her that he ran his family's banking business, but that when he was younger he had been a fashion photographer and had met Ashlyn, who had then been a model.

'I was glad to give up modelling and the lifestyle associated with it,' Ashlyn admitted when she and Leah slipped away to the restroom. 'Now, I feel I should apologise for my husband's lack of tact earlier, when he mentioned Marco's first wife. We both knew her. In fact Karin was a friend of mine in our modelling days, but she was much more sociable and loved to party. It was me who introduced her to Marco.' Ashlyn hesitated. 'I suppose he *has* told you about Karin?'

'A little,' Leah murmured.

But all she really knew was that Marco and his wife had divorced a few years before her untimely death, and she was curious to learn more.

'Marco doesn't like to talk about what happened. He was devastated when Karin went off the way she did—'

Ashlyn broke off as a group of teenage girls entered the restroom, talking and giggling loudly. Leah felt frustrated as she followed the American woman back to the table to join the men and knew there would be no further opportunity to discover more about Nicky's mother.

She felt unsettled by Ashlyn's revelation that Marco had been devastated by the break-up with his wife. She couldn't imagine him *devastated*. He was so enigmatic and guarded in his emotions. Was that because he'd been hurt in the past and had vowed never to risk his heart again?

Leah stared at the gold wedding band on her finger. Her heart missed a beat when Marco leaned across the table and covered her hand with his.

'I see you decided to wear the rose. I'm glad you like it,' he said quietly.

'Was it from you?' She touched the white rose in her hair, and a feeling she could not explain unfurled inside her when he smiled. She tried to remind herself that the rose, like the tourmaline engagement ring, were just props to make their marriage seem believable.

'Your eyes are the colour of the ocean and just as mysterious. What are you thinking, I wonder?' he asked.

The deep melody of his voice felt like a caress over her ultra-sensitive nerve-endings. She couldn't admit to herself, let alone to Marco, that she was jealous of the ghost of his first wife.

'I'm thinking of practicalities,' she told him coolly. 'I need to send a copy of the marriage certificate to the solicitors who are executors of my grandmother's will as soon as possible, so that they will release my inheritance.'

His withdrew his hand and leaned back in his chair, his eyes narrowing on her face. 'How very sensible of you,' he drawled. 'It would not do for either of us to forget the reasons for our marriage.'

CHAPTER EIGHT

IT WAS LATE afternoon when the De Valle private jet took off from Teterboro Airport in New Jersey en route to Italy. Nicky fell asleep almost as soon as they were in the air. He was worn out from his trip to the zoo the previous day and the sleepover—during which, according to Marco's cousin Chiara, none of the children had got much sleep.

Marco carried the little boy into the smaller of the two bedrooms at the rear of the plane and covered him with a blanket before returning to the main cabin, where Leah was sitting on one of the cream leather sofas.

She had slipped off her shoes and tucked her feet beneath her. He paused in the doorway and studied her. The sharp tug of desire in his groin made him catch his breath. His virgin bride was still wearing the sexy dress she'd married him in. Her mix of innocence and sensuality filled Marco with a restlessness which promised that the flight to Naples would be hellishly frustrating.

With any other woman he would have suggested

making use of the plane's master bedroom to create their own in-flight entertainment. But he had vowed that he would resist the chemistry which had simmered between them when they'd been in New York. Presumably Leah had remained a virgin into her twenties because she was looking for something in a relationship—something that he was damned sure *he* couldn't give her, Marco brooded.

It did not help that he was certain she wanted him too. The hungry looks she darted at him when she thought he wouldn't notice would tempt a saint—and he was far from saintly, he acknowledged with a grimace. He had spent the previous evening alone in a bar, and hadn't dared return to the hotel until late, when he'd been sure she had gone to bed.

Leah shifted position, causing her dress to ride up her leg and expose a smooth, toned thigh. Marco imagined pushing the dress up to her waist and slipping his hand into her panties... He cursed silently when his arousal was instant and uncomfortably hard. *Dio*, she made him feel like a teenager with a surfeit of hormones.

He sat down on the sofa opposite her, fascinated by the soft pink stain that ran under her skin as she quickly averted her gaze from him. The stewardess came and served him his customary whisky and soda before retreating to the staff cabin at the front of the plane.

He stretched his long legs out in front of him and took a sip of his drink. 'You have gone to extreme lengths to claim your inheritance,' he murmured. 'What are you planning to do with the money?'

Emotion flickered across Leah's face but was gone before Marco could decipher it.

'I want to buy a house. It's impossible to get on the housing ladder without a decent deposit. My teaching salary isn't huge, and by the time I've paid rent and bills it's hard to save much each month.' She gave a faintly wistful smile. 'I'd like a house with roses growing around the front door.'

'I would have thought you would be more concerned about the location of a property and the number of bedrooms?'

'I don't mind about those things. When I was child I used to look at pictures of houses like that in magazines and pretend that I lived there.'

'You told my aunt that you spent some of your childhood in Italy and can speak the language?'

'Yes.'

Marco felt curious at her reluctance to talk about her childhood. 'You sound as though you did not like living away from England?'

She sighed. 'I had a nomadic childhood.'

'Tell me more,' he said softly when she fell silent.

'Why?'

'Because you are my wife and we are going to spend a year together. I'd like to get to know you better, *cara*.'

It was the truth, Marco realised. Leah intrigued him more than any woman had ever done.

She looked away from him and Marco sensed that

trust was an issue for her—as it was for him, he acknowledged.

After a few moments she gave another sigh. 'When my dad died, I think my mum must have struggled with depression—although I was far too young at the time to realise it. Maybe she wanted to get away from her memories of him, but for whatever reason we moved constantly around Europe, staying with other artists for a few months before moving on to the next place. Eventually we settled at the commune in Tuscany. But even then we didn't have a proper home. The commune members all shared various spaces for sleeping and eating. Eventually we moved back to England and I went to the local comprehensive school, but I found it hard to fit in,' she said ruefully.

Marco pictured Leah as a little girl who longed to call one place home. His own childhood had been very different—structured around term time as a boarder at prep school and then a top English public school. In the holidays he'd stayed at Nancarrow Hall, or with his father's relatives in Capri. But, like Leah, he had wanted to feel a sense of belonging.

Her desire to buy a house that she could call home was understandable, but he couldn't shake off the idea that she was not being completely honest about why she was so desperate for her inheritance.

'Why did you and your mother return to England?'

'My brother was very ill.'

She drew her legs up and hugged her knees. Marco noticed that her toenails were painted a bright coral colour that he found surprising, considering her penchant for all things beige.

'Sammy was two when he was diagnosed with a degenerative neurological disorder which meant that he gradually lost the ability to walk, talk and feed himself. His father—my stepdad—didn't stick around for long, and then there was just me and mum to look after Sammy.'

Marco heard the bite in Leah's voice and guessed she was making a point. She believed he had not tried to keep in contact with Nicky. It wasn't true, he thought bitterly. He had employed private detectives to search for his ex-wife and his son, but Karin had changed her surname in a deliberate ploy to hide Nicky from him.

What a fool he had been, Marco thought savagely, to believe she'd had a change of heart and become willing to allow him to share custody of his son. He'd immediately gone to Mexico to meet Karin, but she had dashed his hopes.

In his mind he heard her sharp voice.

'You can take Nicky to Italy, but you'll have to pay. I'll let you have him for ten million dollars.'

Marco forced his mind away from painful memories as Leah spoke again.

'We moved back to England so that Sammy could receive specialist care, but children with the illness he suffered from rarely live to be teenagers, and he died when he was six.' Her face softened. 'Despite all his problems he was a happy, delightful little boy, and his smile lit up the room.'

'It must have been a difficult time for you and your

mother.' Marco knew his words were inadequate. He understood the pain of loss, but at least he had been reunited with his son. 'You had a huge amount of re-sponsibility put upon you when most girls of your age would have been experimenting with make-up and boyfriends.'

Leah gave a rueful smile. 'Yes, I was too busy help-ing with Sammy and trying to take care of Mum to have time for the normal teenage stuff. I felt older than other people of my age, and I suppose that created a distance between me and my peers.'

'I can understand that,' Marco murmured. 'From the age of seven I knew my destiny was to be CEO of De Valle Caffè—the company my great-grandfather had started, which my grandfather and father had built into a hugely successful brand. When other boys at school were flunking their exams and going out drink-ing I was studying hard and hoping I could live up to the expectations of my family.'

She nodded. 'I think my brother's illness gave me a different perspective on life. I was thirteen when he died. I decided that I wanted to teach, and Sammy was my inspiration to qualify as a special educational needs teacher.'

Marco's eyes met Leah's and they fell silent in a moment of shared empathy. They'd both had to grow up quickly.

'How is your mother now?' he asked. 'Has she been able to come to terms with the tragedies in her life?'

He wondered why Leah suddenly seemed tense, and knew the rapport between them had disappeared.

'Mum has *never* got over losing Sammy. I'll never give up on her, though,' she said in a low voice.

There was a mystery there, Marco brooded, but Leah clearly was not going to explain.

She picked up a magazine from the coffee table and flicked through it. He opened his laptop and tried to concentrate on a financial report, but his awareness of Leah was an unwelcome distraction.

Some time later Marco looked up from his screen and saw that she had fallen asleep. His eyes were drawn to the steady rise and fall of her breasts, framed by the white lace dress. Her cheek was resting on her hand and her lips were slightly parted. She looked as pure as driven snow, and yet at the same time incredibly sexy, with her vibrant hair spilling in silky curls around her shoulders.

Cursing beneath his breath, he stood up and lifted her into his arms. She stirred, but did not wake as he carried her to the double bedroom and laid her on the bed.

He knew the sensible thing to do would be to leave her to sleep and return to the main cabin, to continue working. But right now 'sensible' had never seemed less inviting.

Marco ran his hand around the back of his neck and felt a knot of tension. He'd hardly slept last night—although it had been the knowledge that he was alone in the penthouse with Leah rather than the thunderstorm which had kept him awake. The different time zones between the US and Europe meant that they would

land in Naples at around eight o'clock tomorrow morning, and he knew he should try and get some sleep.

It was not the wedding night he would have planned,
he mused as he kicked off his shoes and lay down next
to his virgin bride. He'd never planned to marry again.
Leah had forced his hand, and he had been angry. But
he had discovered a vulnerability about her as well as
a strong will, he thought ruefully, remembering her
refusal to allow him to buy her clothes.

The unsettling thought struck him that he *liked*
her—which he had not anticipated.

'There's Villa Rosa up ahead.'

Marco pointed towards an enormous pink-walled
house standing on a rocky headland. The undisguised
pleasure in his voice captured Leah's attention. Since
they had boarded the helicopter in Naples, for the short
flight to Capri, he had visibly relaxed.

Her breath snagged in her throat as his mouth
curved in a crooked smile. His eyes were hidden behind designer shades. Dark stubble covered his jaw,
and he looked utterly gorgeous in a pale denim shirt
open at the throat, so that she could see a vee of olive-
gold skin and a sprinkling of black chest hair.

She cast her mind back to earlier that morning,
when she'd woken from a deep sleep and found herself
in the bedroom of his plane which had still been heading to Italy. Her heart had jolted when she'd turned her
head on the pillow and discovered Marco lying next to
her. A blanket had covered both of them. He had been
awake, and there had been a speculative gleam in his

eyes when she'd peeped beneath the blanket and seen her relief that they were both fully clothed.

'You fell asleep and I thought you would be more comfortable on the bed,' he had explained. 'I was tired so I joined you, because Nicky was asleep in the other bedroom.'

Leah had felt herself blush as she'd recalled her erotic dream, in which her hands had been roaming over Marco's body.

'I hope you stayed on your side of the mattress,' she'd muttered, not liking the wicked glint in his eyes.

'*I* did—but you cuddled up to *me* and it was difficult to resist you.'

She'd stared at him in horror. 'Are you saying that we...?'

'*Dio*, what do you take me for?' he'd growled, the amusement disappearing from his eyes. 'Your virtue remains safe.' He'd sprung up from the bed and scowled. 'If I had made love to you I guarantee you would *not* have slept through the experience. When I have sex with a woman I make sure that she is a willing participant—not comatose,' he said bitingly.

But now Marco was clearly in a better mood, and it was easy to understand why as the helicopter flew over the azure sea, sparkling like a precious jewel in the bright sunshine.

'Those rock formations coming out of the sea are called *faraglioni*,' he told her as they flew above three enormous limestone stacks. 'Behind us on the mainland you can see Mount Vesuvius—which is still an active volcano, although it hasn't erupted for many years.'

Minutes later the helicopter landed in the grounds of Villa Rosa and Leah climbed out after Marco. There was a tense moment when they both turned to help Nicky. The little boy hesitated, his eyes on his father, but he put his hand in Leah's.

Marco gave a shrug, but she noticed a nerve flicker in his cheek. If only he had scooped Nicky into his arms and swung him down from the helicopter, she thought. She did not understand why he kept his son at an emotional and physical distance.

They walked through a lush green garden, bejewelled with colourful plants and flowers: purple lavender, shocking pink bougainvillea and vibrant orange lantana. Marco led the way around to the front of the villa, where a steep driveway descended to the road. In every direction there was a panoramic view of the sea and Leah thought it must be the most beautiful place on earth.

'There are roses growing around the front door,' she said with a faint sigh.

Indeed, white roses clambered over the pink walls and framed the entrance, exuding a delicate fragrance that filled the porch.

'My great-grandfather commissioned the villa to be built here on the site of a Roman palace,' Marco explained as he ushered her through the door. 'He named the house after his wife and had the walls painted pink in her honour.'

The interior of the villa was a sumptuous mix of

classic and modern décor, with cool marble floors and vaulted ceilings. Tall windows allowed light to flood in and framed spectacular views of the Bay of Naples. Through a set of French doors Leah saw an infinity pool and a sunbathing terrace, tennis courts and another large garden filled with flowers.

'You have a lovely home,' she murmured, glancing around an elegant but relaxing lounge, which was furnished with big, comfortable-looking sofas. Brightly coloured cushions and rugs added interest to the room, and on a low table was a framed photo of Nicky which must have been taken recently.

Next to it was a photograph of a beautiful woman. The picture was a professional shot and the woman staring directly into the camera was evidently a model. She was stunningly attractive, with long golden hair and slanting brown eyes.

'My ex-wife,' Marco said when he saw Leah staring at the photo. He picked it up and held it out to his son. 'Your *mamma* was pretty and kind and she loved you very much, Nicky,' he said softly.

Was Marco still in love with his first wife?

Leah could not explain why her stomach dipped. According to Ashlyn Bonucci he had been devastated when Karin had left him, which suggested that he hadn't wanted his marriage to end.

They climbed a sweeping staircase and Nicky ran ahead into his toy-filled bedroom. Further along the corridor Marco opened a door and ushered Leah into an airy room decorated in soft blue tones.

'This is your room. If you want anything press the

bell and one of the household staff will come.' He paused on his way out of the door. 'I will be hosting a dinner party this evening. It was arranged a few weeks ago—before I knew that I would be blackmailed into marriage,' he said drily. 'But it will be a useful introduction for you to my social circle. I suggest you wear the red velvet gown.'

When Marco had stepped into the corridor and closed the door behind him, Leah gave in to a childish urge and poked her tongue out at him. Obviously she was relieved that he did not expect her to share his bedroom, she told herself.

Remembering his instruction about what she should wear to dinner she realised she didn't have a choice. It would have to be the velvet dress because she had ignored his order to buy multiple outfits suitable for her role as his wife.

Suddenly her legs felt wobbly and she sank down onto the bed. *She'd done it!* She had met the stipulation in her grandmother's will and emailed the executors a copy of her marriage certificate. Her inheritance had immediately been paid into her bank account, and she'd transferred thirty thousand pounds to the boss of the building firm her mum had taken the money from.

Tori was safe from prosecution and—vitally—had agreed that she needed professional help to overcome her alcoholism.

When Leah had been in Cornwall she'd visited a rehabilitation clinic which had excellent reviews. The Haven offered an intensive therapy program at a residential facility, followed by ongoing support to help its patients live their lives free from addictive substances. The fees were significant, but Leah had told Tori that a legal loophole had allowed her to claim her inheritance without marrying. The lie was better than admitting that she had negotiated a marriage deal with a man she hardly knew.

She inspected her bedroom and discovered a charming en suite bathroom. Her faithful holdall had been brought to her room, and she unzipped it and unpacked the few clothes she'd taken to New York. A door next to the bathroom led into a walk-in wardrobe, and her jaw dropped when she discovered racks of clothes there in her size. There were outfits for daytime and evening, as well as exquisite lingerie and nightgowns.

Leah recognised the dresses were the same ones she'd tried on at the shop on Fifth Avenue. But *she* hadn't bought them. The only explanation was that Marco had given his credit card to the personal stylist and paid for the clothes.

Her temper was simmering as she opened yet another door, expecting to see more storage space. Instead she found herself in an adjoining bedroom. It was a much bigger room than hers, and the colour scheme was an opulent mix of black, gold and rich burgundy. At one end of the room stood an enormous bed with a leather headboard. Her heart missed a beat when she saw a large mirror on the ceiling above the bed. Clearly the master bedroom had been designed for seduction and sex.

'You should be careful, *cara*. If you persist in barging into my bedroom I might think that you want our marriage to be real after all,' Marco drawled. 'Do you like my mirror?'

She swung her startled gaze away from the bed and saw him sprawled in a black leather armchair. Heat swept through her and burned hottest in her feminine core as she pictured them lying on those black satin sheets, their naked bodies reflected in the mirror above them.

She frantically tried to dismiss the erotic images in her mind and make her temper flare in response to his arrogance.

'I'm not here for...for what you're thinking,' she choked. 'I didn't realise that my room is connected to yours. I want an explanation for those clothes in the wardrobe.'

Marco stood up in a lithe movement and crossed the room with long strides, halting in front of her before she had time to retreat back through the door into the safety of her own room. The spicy scent of his cologne teased her senses, but she refused to be overwhelmed by his potent masculinity.

'Well?' she demanded.

'I have explained to you that people will expect my wife to wear haute couture,' he said, sounding bored. 'Think of the clothes as your uniform while you are married to me.'

'I'll pay back every penny of what they cost out of my inheritance.'

Leah bit her lip, aware that without Marco she would not have the means to do so—or to help her mum.

'I can't tell you how relieved I am to finally be able

to claim the money my grandmother left me. I'm grateful for what you have done for me. I intend to keep to my side of our deal, and I'll start working on lesson plans for Nicky straight away.'

Marco gave her a brooding look. 'There is a room next to the playroom which you can use as a classroom. Give me a list of anything you need—books and so on—and I will arrange for them to be delivered.'

He moved back across the room, and Leah released a breath which she hadn't realised until then that she'd been holding.

'I intend to hire a nanny for Nicky,' he said. At her look of surprise he went on smoothly, 'Your role is to be his teacher. I don't expect you to care for Nicky all the time. For one thing you will have duties to fulfil as my wife—being my social hostess and accompanying me to business functions,' he explained drily when she frowned. 'However, I'll have to ask you to look after Nicky until I have found a suitable nanny.'

She nodded. 'Of course. But what about you? It doesn't sound like you plan to spend much time with him.'

A shadow flickered across Marco's face. 'Nicky will respond better to a nanny. You have seen how he shies away from me,' he said grimly.

'That's because you're a stranger to him.' Leah could not hide her frustration. 'You and I both know what it was like to lose a parent when we were children. Put yourself in Nicky's shoes. His world was destroyed when he lost his mother. He was thrown into a new life in a strange country with *you*—the father

he doesn't know. You've asked me to help Nicky overcome his problems. I'm beginning to think that *you*
are the biggest problem.'

She should not have blamed Marco, Leah thought,
much later that night. His stern features hadn't revealed a glimmer of emotion when she'd suggested
that he was to blame for his strained relationship with
Nicky, but she'd sensed that he had been hurt.

He was an impossible man to understand.

She hadn't spoken to him for the rest of the day.
Exploring the villa and its grounds had taken up the
morning, and Nicky had nodded enthusiastically when
she'd suggested swimming in the pool after lunch. She
knew he couldn't swim, and one of the staff had found
a pair of inflatable armbands for the little boy to wear.

Leah hadn't packed swimwear when she'd left Nancarrow Hall in a hurry. But in her wardrobe she had
discovered a selection of gorgeous bikinis. They were
much skimpier than anything she would have chosen,
and she had felt self-conscious when she'd realised that
Marco's study overlooked the pool and he might have
been watching her and Nicky through the window.

He had come into Nicky's bedroom as she was reading him a bedtime story that evening. She'd left him to
say goodnight to the little boy and gone to her room to
change for the dinner party. Now, butterflies danced in
her stomach as she applied more make-up than usual
and bundled her hair into a reasonably neat chignon
before stepping into the red velvet gown.

When she walked into the drawing room Marco

said nothing for several long seconds while his eyes roamed over her. He looked stunning in a dinner suit and black silk shirt, and Leah's heart thudded as he strolled towards her, holding a rose with a short stem in his fingers.

'*Sei bellissima,*' he said, tucking the rose into her hair. 'But you are nervous,' he murmured when he stroked his thumb over her bottom lip and felt a betraying quiver.

'This is not my world,' she whispered.

The grandeur of the villa, the discreet but obvious signs of huge wealth, even the designer dress she was wearing, made her feel like an imposter.

'It is for the next year.' Marco lifted her hand and pressed his lips against the gold wedding band beside the tourmaline ring on her finger. His eyes glinted. 'You made your bed and now you must lie in it, *cara.*'

In fact the dinner party was not the ordeal Leah had dreaded. If any of Marco's guests were surprised when he introduced her as his wife, they were far too well-mannered to comment. It helped that she was able to chat to them in Italian, and during the evening she had felt her confidence grow.

There had been a moment when she'd glanced across the table and found Marco watching her. She'd imagined what it would be like if their marriage was real. Would they both be impatient for the party to end so that they could spend the rest of the night making love in that decadent bedroom with the mirror above the bed?

Now it was almost midnight, and Marco and the

household staff had retired for the night. But Leah's body clock hadn't adapted to the different time zone and she could not sleep. She slid out of bed and knelt on the window seat. The night was clear, and a full moon dappled the sea with its silvery gleam.

Suddenly a cry that sounded like an animal in pain rent the air. It was a chilling noise, and Leah's blood froze when it came again, raw and agonised, from the other side of the connecting door. Could Marco be ill?

Biting her lip, she stood by the door and listened. He was shouting in a harsh voice that grew louder and more urgent.

'Karin! Come back!'

CHAPTER NINE

'IT'S JUST A dream.' Wake up, Marco!'

A hand on his shoulder…shaking him. A soft voice… Leah's voice.

Marco opened his eyes and saw her pretty face close to his as she leaned over the bed. He realised that she had switched on the bedside lamp. He shoved his hair off his brow with an unsteady hand. His mind was still trapped in the nightmare of Karin driving away with his son.

'Nicky…'

'I looked in on Nicky about half an hour ago. He's fast asleep. Lucky him. My internal clock can't work out if it's day or night and I'm wide awake.'

Leah spoke in a light voice and Marco realised that she was trying to distract his thoughts from the dream.

He sat upright and met her concerned gaze. Her green eyes were deep enough to drown in, and he wanted to lose himself in her and forget the images in his head, the fear that he could still taste in his mouth.

'Do you want a drink?' She picked up the glass of water from the bedside table and held it to his lips.

The simple, caring gesture shocked him. Tenderness had not been a feature of his childhood—his mother had married his father for money and had dutifully produced the next De Valle heir. The only time Marco had received anything like affection had been at boarding school, when the matron there had been briskly sympathetic after he'd broken his collarbone playing rugby.

When he'd met Karin, sex had lured him into believing that physical intimacy was love—but he'd quickly realised his mistake.

He leaned back against the headboard and watched Leah set the glass back down. As she perched on the edge of the bed her blue satin negligee rode up to reveal her slim thighs. Marco was wide awake now, and his hunger for her was a ravenous beast.

'I'm guessing your nightmare was about the accident,' she murmured. 'Would it help to talk about it?'

'I don't want to *talk*.'

He watched her eyes widen with the awareness that had simmered between them all evening. When she'd looked at him during dinner the naked longing in her eyes had made him instantly hard. If they had been alone he would have been tempted to sweep away the china and glass so that he could make love to her on the polished mahogany dining table.

A pink stain ran under her skin and the pulse at the base of her throat jerked erratically. 'I should go,' she said in a low voice.

But she remained sitting there on his bed as he leaned towards her. She flicked her tongue over her lips and Marco's gut clenched. Her skin was the co-lour of pale cream, dusted with tiny golden freckles. He wanted to taste each one.

Out in the hallway the clock struck midnight. The witching hour—and he was bewitched.

She shivered when he ran his finger over the nar-row strap of her nightgown. 'Pretty,' he growled as he slid the strap a little way down her arm and brushed his lips over her bare shoulder.

'Marco...' she whispered, with uncertainty in her voice and something else that made his need darker and more dangerous.

'You came to my room, *cara*.'

'I heard you call out. You sounded—' Leah broke off.

Marco guessed it had been bad. His throat felt raw and he remembered that in the dream he had been shouting. Snatches of the nightmare returned. The car with Nicky inside. Smoke and flames as he fought to open the door and save his son.

'I thought there might be something I could do to help you.'

Leah's voice pulled him from the darkness of his thoughts.

'There is.'

He leaned even closer to her and sank his hands into her glorious hair. And then he did what he had wanted to do for ever, it seemed. He kissed her.

Her soft sigh filled his mouth and the sweet taste of her made him groan. He fell back against the pil-lows, pulling her down with him, his lips not leaving hers for a second. Her riotous curls cascaded around them like a fragrant curtain and he wound his fingers through the silky strands, angling her head so that he could kiss her again and again.

And she let him. More than let him, Marco thought, aware of an odd feeling inside him when she parted her lips beneath his. He told himself the feeling was satisfaction that he finally had her where he wanted her—in his bed.

He rolled her onto her back and stretched out next to her, propping himself up on one elbow. Her breasts rose and fell jerkily, and a flush of sexual warmth spread down her neck and décolletage.

'Tell me what you want,' he commanded. 'For me to kiss you here?' He pressed his lips to the little hollow behind her ear and heard her draw a shaky breath. 'Or here?' He trailed kisses down her cheek to the corner of her mouth.

'Yes.'

The simple honesty of her surrender stormed through him and Marco reminded himself that this was about sex—nothing more. He traced his mouth over the slopes of her breasts to the lacy edge of her negligee and untied the ribbon that held the front together. Slowly he pushed the satin aside and bared the breasts that he'd fantasised about far too often. He exhaled heavily as he studied the perfect roundness of her pale breasts tipped with rosy nipples.

'Ah, beauty…' He hardly recognised his own voice, so thick was it—so slurred with desire, as if he'd been drugged.

He had never wanted any woman as desperately as he wanted Leah. The realisation set an alarm bell ringing in his mind, but he could not resist the siren song of her body, and he liked it too much when a shiver ran through her as he cupped one creamy mound in his palm and bent his head to draw the stiff peak at its centre into his mouth.

The low moan she made tore through him. Surely his virgin bride could not be *such* an innocent? But he sensed that this was all new for her, and felt something worryingly like possessiveness surge through him.

If he was a better man he would send her back through the connecting door and advise her to keep it locked from now on. But the scent of her teased his senses: a delicate floral perfume mixed with the earthy sweetness of her feminine arousal. His body felt taut with need, but Leah needed careful handling and he was determined not to rush her.

Leah sucked in a breath. She was shaking, and every inch of her body felt too hot, too needy. Marco's hands were everywhere—cupping her breasts, then sliding down over her stomach and thighs. She had not even been aware of him removing her negligee. His fingertips traced patterns over her skin and every caress made the fire inside her burn hotter.

When he flicked his thumb-pad across the hard peak of one nipple, and then its twin, she twisted her hips restlessly, wanting to be even closer to him, desperate for him to assuage the ache deep in her pelvis.

'Touch me.'

The rasp of his voice made the trembling in her limbs worse. She placed her hands on his chest and felt the uneven thud of his heart. He was all muscle and sinew, darkly tanned skin and whorls of black chest hair that arrowed over his taut abdomen and disappeared beneath the sheet draped low over his hips.

The idea that he might be naked beneath the sheet made her heart thud harder. But her thoughts scattered when he slipped his hand between her thighs and stroked his finger over the lace panel of her knickers. An age-old instinct took over and she arched against his hand, needing more, needing—

'Oh...' A shudder ran through her as he pushed her panties aside so that he had access to the molten heart of her femininity. The wetness between her legs betrayed her. She could no longer deny that she desired him, and she caught her breath as he stroked his finger up and down her opening before he parted her and slid in deep.

It felt different from when she touched herself. It was shockingly intimate and utterly addictive as he began to move his hand in a rhythmic motion: pressing forward, withdrawing, pressing, withdrawing... Ripples tightened across her belly as pleasure built inside her. She closed her eyes, her entire being focused on the slide of his finger.

He rubbed his thumb-pad against the hard nub of her core and she shattered. It was indescribable—starbursts of glorious sensation so intense that it almost hurt. She'd read about mind-blowing orgasms, but this was so much more than she'd imagined—emotionally as well as physically.

She felt closer to Marco than she'd ever felt to any other human being, and gave a sigh of protest when he rolled away from her.

'I'm not going far, *cara*.'

His voice was indulgent, and the satisfaction Leah heard in his tone evoked a faint unease when he murmured, 'I assume you want *me* to take care of protection?'

Her eyes flew open and she stared at their reflection in the mirror above the bed. She did not recognise that wanton woman with her wild red hair spread across the pillows, naked apart from the strip of blue lace between her legs that had not been any barrier to Marco's bold caresses.

How had she got here?

A memory pushed through the fog of sexual delight. In her mind she heard Marco shouting a name. *Karin*.

He was opening the bedside drawer and taking out a packet of condoms. The cold reality of the situation doused Leah like a shower of ice. She had been compelled by Marco's haunting cries to rush into his room and wake him from his nightmare. When he'd kissed her she'd gone up in flames. But she was not the woman he wanted.

'No!' She jerked upright and grabbed her negligee, dragging it inelegantly over her head.

'No?' Marco's eyes narrowed until they were gleaming slits of polished steel, but he did not move towards her or try to prevent her from scrambling across the bed away from him. 'That's not the message you gave me a few minutes ago.'

'I won't be a substitute for your first wife.'

He stiffened and jerked his head back, shock and another indefinable emotion chasing across his stern features.

Silence stretched between them, simmering with tension.

'You called out for Karin in your dream,' Leah muttered.

While Marco had been kissing her, had he been thinking of his beautiful wife, whose photograph he kept in every room of his home?

'I'm not her.'

He laughed then, but it was an oddly harsh sound that held no humour. 'No. You are certainly *not* her.'

She caught her lower lip between her teeth as she tied the ribbon at the front of her negligee with hands that visibly trembled. She felt vulnerable and exposed—humiliated when she thought of how he'd watched her in the throes of orgasm.

With a muffled cry she went to stand up, but he caught hold of her arm and tugged her back down onto the bed.

'Leah. You are the only woman I want right now.' Marco feathered his fingertips along her collarbone. 'You feel the attraction between us as much as I do,' he murmured in a molten honey voice as he held his thumb over the pulse thudding at the base of her throat. 'This fire is not going to burn out any time soon.'

But all fires died when there was nothing to feed

the flames, Leah thought. The spark of desire Marco felt for her would not last long.

He bent his dark head and she felt the silken brush of his hair on her skin as he pressed his lips against the side of her neck. 'You want to give yourself to me, beauty.'

So confident. So sure of himself—and of her. But she wasn't gullible, as her mother had been too often with lovers who had promised everything and given nothing.

'No,' she said firmly, pulling away from him and sliding off the bed. 'Sex isn't part of our deal.'

She sped into her own room as if the hounds of hell were snapping at her heels. As she shut the door she heard Marco's lazy drawl.

'It will be, *cara*. A year is a long time to fight the raging desire we both feel.'

The sound of the helicopter flying over Villa Rosa sent Leah's stomach into a nose-dive. She had learned from the housekeeper, Assumpta, that Marco was coming home today. It would have been nice if he'd phoned her and told her of his plans, she thought with a grimace. But he hadn't been in contact for the past week, since he'd left Capri to go on a business trip.

She had dreaded facing him at breakfast the morning after she'd gone into his room. Memories of how he had seduced her with his addictive kisses and pleasured her with his wickedly inventive hands had made her shudder with shame. But the butterflies in her stomach had been for nothing.

Signor De Valle had left in the helicopter very early, Assumpta had explained.

Now, Leah collected up the number cards she had been using to test Nicky's numeracy skills. 'That's enough sums for today. I think your *papà* has arrived. Are you looking forward to seeing him?'

Nicky nodded, and his shy smile tugged on her heart.

Every afternoon they went to the pool, so that she could teach him to swim. Supporting his little body while he kicked his legs reminded her of being in the hydrotherapy pool with her brother. Sammy had loved those sessions with the physiotherapist, but as his illness had progressed he'd become too weak to swim.

Being with Nicky was helping to mend the hole that had ripped open Leah's heart when Sammy had died. But her role in Nicky's life was not permanent, and it was important that he developed a trusting relationship with his father. Sadly that was impossible when Marco was never around.

'Let's go and see if Assumpta has your lunch ready,' she said to the little boy. 'Maybe your *papà* will come swimming this afternoon?'

He would if *she* had anything to do with it, she vowed a short while later, as she tried to ignore the frantic thud of her heart and knocked on the study door.

At his curt command she stepped into the room. Marco was on his phone, of course. He looked over at her and the predatory hunger in his eyes was shockingly exciting. Heat flared in her belly and she felt a betraying blush spread over her cheeks.

He finished the call and leaned back in his chair. 'Don't hover as if you're planning to scamper out of the door like a frightened rabbit. I'm not going to bite you,' he drawled.

She ground her teeth as she sat down on the chair in front of his desk. 'I'm here to discuss your son,' Leah said stiffly. 'And to show you this.'

She pushed a piece of paper on which Nicky had drawn a picture of his father across the desk.

A nerve flickered in Marco's cheek as he stared at the childish representation of himself. In the picture, the jagged line running down his face was obviously meant to be his scar. Nicky had scribbled it in red crayon over the paper.

'I asked him if the red was meant to be blood and he became upset,' Leah said quietly.

'What does it mean? Why did Nicky draw this?'

'I don't know. I'm not a psychotherapist.' She leaned across the desk and held Marco's gaze. 'But I know Nicky needs to spend more time with you. I am convinced that his problems are linked to his relationship, or lack of one, with *you*. He needs you to be more involved with him.'

Leah gave a sigh of frustration when Marco stood up abruptly and strode over to the window.

She stared at his stiff back. 'Don't you *want* to be closer to Nicky?'

'Of course I do,' he said, in an agonised voice that tugged at Leah's heart.

He spun round and glared at her, and she was startled by the raw emotion on his face. His skin was drawn tight over his cheekbones and his scar was a livid white mark standing out against his olive complexion.

'I don't know how to be a good father.'

'You had a good relationship with your own father, didn't you?' she probed gently.

'I didn't spend much time with him, to be honest. He worked away for weeks at a time, and when he came back to Nancarrow Hall he was mainly interested in talking to me about the business. He used to joke that he was training me early to take his place.' Marco shrugged. 'Perhaps he had a premonition that he would die young.'

Leah remembered Marco had told her that after his father had died and his mother had remarried he had been sent away to school.

'Who ran the company until you were old enough to be CEO?' she asked.

'Tia Benedetta's late husband—Tio Federico.' Marco's face softened 'He was a good, kind man and he treated me like the son he never had.'

'*You* have a son.' Leah was too agitated to remain sitting, and she jumped up and walked around the desk. 'I implore you to make time for Nicky. You are the only parent he has and you must be the hands-on father he is so desperate for—starting from now.'

'You don't understand.' A nerve jumped in his cheek. 'When Nicky was inside the wreckage after the accident I could smell petrol. I was scared the car would catch fire before I could save him.' Marco swallowed convulsively. 'Finally I managed to get the door open. Nicky was wearing a seat belt, but he was limp and grey and I believed he was dead.'

Leah's heart clenched. The horror of the accident had left Marco traumatised as well as Nicky, she realised. But Marco's way of dealing with his emotions was to ignore them.

'Are you afraid to love your son because you can't bear the idea of losing him to another accident or a serious illness?' she said softly.

His jaw clenched. 'How the hell can you know that?'

'When my brother died it hurt so much I never wanted to love anyone again. But none of us can live our lives in fear of what might happen in the future. Nicky needs to know that you love him.'

'I don't think he likes me.' Marco ran his fingers through his hair until it stood on end.

'He doesn't *know* you.' Leah put her hand on Marco's arm. 'Take some time off work, turn off your laptop and phone and give fatherhood a chance.'

His eyes locked with hers, and Leah felt as though her heart was being squeezed when he said gruffly, 'I need you to help me.'

'I will. We made a deal, remember?' she said lightly, trying to ease the tension.

He gave her a speculative look. 'I am hardly likely to forget, *cara*.'

This was a different Marco. He was allowing her to see the man behind the mask and revealing that he was vulnerable—at least where his son was concerned.

When she had believed him to be cold and heartless it had been easier to tell herself that her awareness of him was a purely physical response, Leah thought ruefully. But now she had discovered that he was a complex man and her feelings for him were complicated.

She suddenly wished that they had met in the normal way and been attracted to each other without the marriage negotiation which was a barrier between them. Instead she was his wife in name only. Which was what she wanted—wasn't it?

CHAPTER TEN

FOR THE FIRST few days he did not go to his office in Naples, Marco felt cut adrift from the life he'd known since he was twenty-one. The responsibility of heading the family company, which had been entrusted to him, had dominated his waking hours for the past fourteen years, and he was the first to admit that he wasn't good at delegating.

But he was doing it—and slowly he was starting to see the rewards.

That first afternoon when he'd joined Leah and Nicky in the pool had been strained. His son had been wary of him, reinforcing Marco's conviction that he wasn't a natural father. He'd felt a fool, frankly, standing in the shallow end of the pool while he tried to coax Nicky to leave Leah's side.

'Talk to him about what?' he'd muttered, when she had suggested he tried to have a conversation with the little boy.

'Tell him about the things you used to do when you were his age,' she advised. 'Use your imagination.'

At the time his imagination had had him visualising untying the strings of her halter-neck bikini and peeling the gold triangles of material away from her breasts. Silently cursing his out-of-control libido, he'd searched his mind for something to say to his son.

'When I was a boy I lived in England, in that big old house where you fell in the lake.'

It hadn't been the best start, Marco admitted, recalling how he'd scolded Nicky then. He remembered that Leah had been furious with him as she'd sprung to his son's defence.

'My *papà* used to take me out on that lake in a boat,' he'd told Nicky.

Memories had surfaced of times when he and his father had gone fishing together. Happy memories that he'd forgotten, or maybe buried inside him when his father had died so suddenly. And Marco had realised that he had a lot to tell his son about Vincenzo De Valle—Nicky's grandfather.

Two weeks had passed since then, and there had been a huge improvement in Marco's relationship with Nicky. The little boy no longer shied away from him, and he seemed more relaxed when they were together—which was often.

Marco had discovered a world of train sets, toy cars and Nicky's favourite books. Goals had been erected on the lawn so they could play football, and daily sessions in the pool meant that Nicky could now swim without water wings.

Things were good—but they would be even better if Marco wasn't so sexually frustrated that he was climbing the walls.

He glanced over his shoulder to the stern of the motor cruiser, where Leah was sitting with Nicky. The little boy loved going on the boat, and they were returning from a trip to visit the famous Blue Grotto. As they sped over the waves the breeze blew Leah's red curls around her face and she laughed and caught her hair in her hand, winding it up and securing it with a clip on top of her head.

She became more beautiful every day, Marco mused. Her skin had gained a light tan, and he now knew that the golden freckles on her nose and cheeks were also sprinkled over her breasts.

That night she'd come to his room to wake him from his nightmare was constantly in his mind. Her gorgeous body had been so responsive to his caresses, and her soft cries as she'd climaxed beneath his hand had fuelled his desire. He hadn't trusted himself to be near her and had left the villa early the next morning, having requested his PA to reschedule a business trip to Germany and make it start immediately.

Since he had returned to the villa the connecting door between his room and Leah's had remained closed. Marco had spent sleepless nights, his body aching with frustration.

He knew Leah was aware of the sexual chemistry between them—it was almost tangible. And if she hadn't been a virgin he might have tried to seduce her into his bed. But her innocence held him back. She deserved more than he could give her, and he sensed that for Leah desire would be inextricably linked with deeper emotions—like love.

In every other respect she was proving to be an ideal wife. She had accompanied him to dinner parties given by his friends in Capri and Positano, and looked stunning dressed in designer gowns. But Marco preferred her as she was now, wearing frayed denim shorts that revealed her toned thighs and a tight-fitting T-shirt that moulded her firm breasts.

No bra, he noted, his gaze lingering on the outline of her nipples.

Desire corkscrewed through him and he tore his gaze from her and concentrated on driving the boat.

It was not long before they reached the private beach belonging to Villa Rosa, and after he'd secured the boat with a rope tied to a mooring post he jumped onto the jetty and turned to help Leah and Nicky disembark. The little boy ran ahead of them up the steep driveway.

'Nicky, wait!' Marco called as a delivery truck rumbled past on its way to the house. He glanced at Leah. 'I've left my sunglasses on the boat. You go on with Nicky while I run back for them.'

He jogged down the driveway and was almost at the bottom of the incline when he heard Leah scream.

'Marco, look out!'

Glancing over his shoulder, he saw the truck hurtling towards him. He realised in seconds, as it gained momentum, that the driver must have turned the vehicle at the top of the hill and parked, but couldn't have applied the handbrake properly. The driver was not behind the wheel, and the truck was almost upon Marco.

With nowhere else to go, he leapt over the wall and

swore as he half fell, half scrambled down the rocky cliff before landing on a ledge. From above him he heard a crash, and guessed that the truck must have hit the wall.

His arms were covered in scratches from the brambles, and no doubt he would find bruises on his body, but he'd been lucky. If Leah hadn't alerted him the truck would have ploughed into him.

He hauled himself back up the cliff and hooked a leg over the wall to climb over it.

'*Papà! Papà!*'

Marco turned his head towards the house and saw Nicky, chased by Leah, running down the driveway. The little boy was sobbing hysterically.

'*Papà!*'

His son's distress tore at Marco's heart. Nicky had not cried since the accident, but now tears poured down his cheeks.

'Nicky, it's okay,' he said huskily, hunkering down and wrapping his arms around his son's quivering body.

Nicky stared at him. 'You went away and another man came,' he choked through his tears.

'Do you mean at the hospital? I was there with you, Nicky. But maybe I looked different,' Marco said slowly, as he began to comprehend why his son seemed afraid of him.

He glanced at Leah.

'After the accident I had to leave Nicky in the children's ward while my cheek was stitched up. My face was covered in bandages for days, but it never occurred to me that Nicky might have thought I was a stranger. I must have looked terrifying to a child. It would have been another trauma on top of everything else he'd been through.'

Marco touched his scar and grimaced when he discovered the blood on his face.

'You've got a nasty cut above your eyebrow,' Leah told him.

Nicky was still crying, and Marco put his hands on his son's shoulders. 'It wasn't another man at the hospital, it was *me*, Nicky. My face looks different, but I am still your *papà*.'

Marco swallowed hard. He did not find it easy to reveal his emotions, but Leah had been right when she'd said Nicky needed to know that his father cared about him.

'You are my son and I love you,' he said softly. 'I will always love you, and everything is going to be okay.'

This time when he drew Nicky towards him the little boy wriggled closer. Marco pressed his face against his son's dark curls and felt tears burn his eyes. He looked at the smashed wall and the crumpled front end of the truck and knew he might have been killed if the truck had hit him.

Life was infinitely precious. He could never regain those first years of his son's life that he'd missed, but thanks to Leah he had a lifetime with Nicky ahead of him.

'I think we need ice-cream,' he said gruffly as he stood up and lifted Nicky into his arms.

He looked at Leah and saw a tear slide down her cheek. Her emotional response evoked an odd tug in his chest. Seeing her with his son for the past weeks had been a revelation. She was compassionate, and her beauty was much more than skin-deep.

It was becoming harder and harder to remember that she had blackmailed him into marriage. The situation between them couldn't continue. He was going out of his mind with wanting her.

'Thank you,' he said quietly as they walked back to the house.

She shook her head. 'I didn't do anything.'

'You saved my life. I didn't hear the truck because its engine wasn't running. More importantly, you have shown me how to connect with my son.'

'You've won Nicky's trust by spending time with him. You're a good father, Marco.'

Her smile stole his breath, and he felt a tug beneath his breastbone so intense that he pressed his hand against his chest.

'A couple of bruised ribs,' he lied when she looked concerned. He looked at his watch. 'The nanny will be arriving soon. I employed Silvana when I first brought Nicky to Capri, and since her father has passed away she is happy to come back to Villa Rosa. Silvana will take care of Nicky while we go to Rome.'

'We?'

She stared at him and he saw a mutinous expression replace her smile. They had reached the house, and Nicky ran inside. Leah stood in the entrance, framed by the profusion of white roses that clambered around the front door. Once again Marco pressed his palm to his chest and felt the erratic thud of his heart.

'Assumpta has told me that you are going away for the weekend. I wondered when you were going to mention it,' she said pointedly. 'But I'm not coming with you.'

'The annual charity ball sponsored by De Valle Caffè is the most prestigious event in the company's calendar, and it attracts the support of businesses and celebrities from all over Europe. You are the new wife of the CEO and it will look odd to the board members and shareholders if you are not with me. If there is any hint of a scandal the paparazzi will hound us, and negative publicity could harm the company.' Marco ignored the glitter in Leah's green eyes. 'In fact, I think we should practise showing a united front to the cameras.'

'Practise how?' she said suspiciously.

'Like this.'

He lowered his head until his lips were centimetres from hers and watched her green eyes darken to the colour of a stormy sea. Something held him back from claiming her mouth.

A memory slid into his mind of that time when she had suggested he might force her to sleep with him. She'd dented his pride then, and now he needed to be sure she was caught in the same web of desire that held him prisoner.

'Marco…'

The husky plea in her voice shattered his control and he brushed his mouth over hers gently, taking his time to savour her soft sigh of surrender. Only then did he coax her lips apart with the tip of his tongue.

She tasted like nectar, and the heady fragrance of her perfume mingled with the scent of the roses and teased his senses. Passion exploded between them as he deepened the kiss until she melted against him and her lips clung to his.

The sound of someone shouting made him reluctantly lift his head, and he glanced up and saw the delivery driver running around the corner of the house.

Leah's face was flushed, and Marco ran his knuckles over her peachy skin. 'That wasn't bad,' he drawled, deliberately teasing her to stop himself from throwing her over his shoulder, caveman-style, and carrying her to his bed. 'But you'll need more practice at kissing if you're going to convince the public that you are besotted with your husband.'

He laid his finger across her lips. He could see from the furious glint in her eyes that an angry retort was about to burst forth. She sank her teeth into his finger and he cursed.

'Wildcat. Be ready to leave in an hour.'

Hunger was a vicious beast, clawing in his gut.

'And know this: bite me again and you'll have to be prepared for the consequences, beauty.'

The party was the most spectacular event Leah had ever attended and then some. It was held in the ballroom of the most exclusive hotel in Rome, and the great and the good of the Eternal City had gathered there beneath glittering chandeliers to drink champagne and feast on exquisite canapés.

An auction had raised a phenomenal amount of money for various charities, and Marco had given a moving speech about the work of a charity for homeless children which was close to his heart.

Leah's gaze had been riveted on him as he'd stood there on the podium. He looked breathtaking, in a black dinner suit that moulded his muscular frame. But she wasn't the only woman to be fantasising about loosening his bow tie and ripping open the buttons on his white silk shirt, she'd realised, when she'd noticed the admiring looks that practically every female in the room sent him.

But he was hers—in public, at least.

She was shocked by the fierce possessiveness she felt. He'd told her that they must act like happy newlyweds and she had thrown herself into the role, offering no resistance when he slipped his arm around her waist and held her close against his side as they strolled around the room and mingled with the other guests.

While a buffet was being served in another room the hotel staff cleared the ballroom of the tables where people had sat for the auction. Soon the band struck up, and Marco swept Leah into his arms and led her onto the dance floor.

'You have never looked more beautiful than you do tonight,' he murmured, his warm breath stirring the tendrils of curls that framed her face.

She wore the front of her hair up and had left the back loose. The white rose that Marco had given her was tucked into her hair. Her heart missed a beat when he wound a long curl around his finger. She wanted to say something flippant in response to his compliment, but the gleam in his eyes as he looked intently at her made her feel beautiful.

Her strapless sea-green silk evening gown felt sensuous against her skin as Marco whirled her around the ballroom. The diamond earrings dangling from her earlobes and the diamonds at her throat must be worth a fortune. She had protested about wearing them when he'd presented the jewellery to her after she'd emerged from her bedroom in the penthouse suite of the hotel where they were staying for the weekend.

'Humour me, hmm?' he'd drawled as he'd fastened the clasp of the necklace and pressed his lips to the side of her throat.

A quiver had run through her and she'd accepted that trying to resist him was futile.

She wanted to make love with him. It was as simple and uncomplicated as that.

When she'd watched that delivery truck roll down the driveway and realised that Marco was unaware of the danger he was in she had been terrified. In those horrifying moments her thoughts had clarified into a stark truth. She could no longer deny her desire for him.

Tonight's glamorous party was *his* world, not hers, but their hunger for each other made them equal.

She did not fool herself that he loved her—which was what her mother had done every time she'd begun another affair. And Leah assured herself that she had more sense than to lose her heart to Marco. But she liked him, and she felt safe with him. Not safe in the way her passionless relationship with James had made her feel. Marco had shown her that her difficult childhood had made her strong and that she could handle a sexual relationship with him. That sometimes being in control was about knowing when to let go.

The tempo of the music changed to a slow number and Marco pulled her close, so that she felt the hard ridge of his arousal nudge her thigh. He smelled divine: of spicy cologne and another indefinable scent that was excitingly *male*. With a faint sigh she rested her head on his chest and heard the powerful thud of his heart. He brushed his lips over her shoulder, sending a shiver of reaction through her.

She realised that he'd been flirting with her all evening, taking every opportunity to caress her with a hand stroking her bare back or his mouth brushing over her cheek. He was clearly intent on seducing her. But instead of pulling away from him she pressed her pelvis against his and heard him groan.

'You are driving me insane,' he said thickly. 'How much longer are you going to make me wait, *cara mia*?'

Fire licked through her. 'Well, I suppose we should stay here in the ballroom until the party ends at midnight as you are the host…'

'Like hell we should.'

He stopped dancing and clamped her to his side as he strode towards the exit.

'Won't you be missed?' she murmured when he ushered her into a lift.

'I don't give a damn.'

He leaned back against the lift wall and pulled her towards him, one hand splaying over her bottom, the other tugging at his bow tie. His urgency heightened her anticipation and her pulse quickened when the door opened directly into the penthouse suite.

She'd expected Marco to lead her straight to the master bedroom, and butterflies had taken up residence in her stomach. But he strode across the sitting room and opened the sliding glass doors that led out onto the balcony. Rome was spread out before them, a blaze of lights against an inky sky.

Leah followed him over to where he stood beside the balcony rail.

'Why did you want your inheritance so badly?' he asked. 'Was it really to get on the property ladder, as you told me?'

His curiosity took her by surprise. She bit her lip. 'Does it matter why?'

'You must have had plans for how to spend the money if you were prepared to marry a virtual stranger to get your hands on it,' he said harshly. 'But everything I've learned about you indicates that you are not money-driven.'

He gently captured her chin between his lean fingers and tilted her face up so that her gaze collided with his.

'Leah, do you trust me?'

Her breath left her on a long sigh as she realised that

she did. Trust did not come easily to her, but Marco had been devastatingly honest when he'd confided that he did not know how to be a father to his son.

'I needed the money for my mother. I've done my best to look after her for most of my life,' she admitted.

Marco said nothing and his eyes did not leave her face.

'Mum is…an alcoholic. She's always liked a drink, but after my brother died she started drinking heavily.'

Leah tensed, expecting Marco to be disgusted or judgemental—which were the reactions she'd had in the past if she ever spoke about her mum's reliance on alcohol.

'It must have been difficult when you were growing up—having to be responsible for a parent when she should have been the one taking care of you,' he suggested.

She nodded. 'I felt helpless. I didn't want anyone at school to know that my mum was different to other mothers, or that a normal weekend for me was to find Mum passed out on the bathroom floor. I used to get up early to take the empty vodka bottles to the bottle bank so that no one would see me.'

Leah sighed.

'Despite everything I know Mum loves me—and I love her. She is all I have. The inheritance money is paying for her to be treated at a private clinic.' She gave Marco a faint smile. 'Mum is halfway through the programme and she's doing well.'

'*Dio!* Why didn't you just borrow the amount you needed to pay for your mother's treatment?'

She gave him a wry look. 'Would *you* have agreed to give me a loan? Especially as I had no way of paying it back? And my mother had other problems which needed to be resolved quickly.'

Leah's voice faltered, but she realised that Marco was waiting patiently for her to continue, and she felt a sense of relief in unburdening herself of the worry she'd felt that her mum could go to prison.

'Mum stole some money from the company she worked for and I needed to repay it before the police got involved.'

He swore softly. 'So you negotiated a marriage deal with a man you barely knew?'

'I didn't know what else I could do. You were my only hope of helping my mother.'

Marco nodded. 'But we are no longer strangers.'

The expression in his eyes made Leah's heart lurch. 'Do you want to make our marriage real?' she whispered.

'What I want from you, *cara*, is your honesty.'

CHAPTER ELEVEN

'I want to have sex with you. Is that honest enough?'

Leah followed Marco into his bedroom and watched him shrug off his jacket and unfasten the top few buttons on his shirt.

'Prove it.'

He sat on the bed and leaned back against the headboard, folding his arms behind his head. His eyes gleamed as he raked them over her like a sultan inspecting his favourite concubine.

Once she might have turned tail and fled. But she wasn't that person any more. She knew what she wanted and she was prepared to fight for it.

With sudden insight Leah understood that Marco needed to be sure she was coming to him willingly. Her heart contracted.

'If you don't make love to me tonight, I think I'll go out of my mind,' she said huskily.

'I've spent the evening fantasising about you wearing those diamonds and nothing else,' he growled.

His voice had roughened, and Leah felt a thrill of

feminine triumph when she realised that he wasn't as relaxed as he wanted her to think.

'I'll fulfil your fantasies if you promise to fulfil mine.'

His sexy smile set her pulse racing. 'Be careful what you wish for, beauty.'

She ran her tongue over her dry lips. The time for talking was over.

Reaching behind her, she ran the zip of her dress down her spine. The green silk fell away from her breasts and slipped down her body to pool at her feet.

Marco sat upright and his breath hissed between his teeth.

Carefully she stepped away from the dress and kicked off her stilettos. The only remaining item of clothing was her black lace knickers. She hesitated for a second, and then hooked her fingers into the top and pulled them down.

Leah's nerve faltered when she was finally naked in front of Marco and feeling self-conscious of her body's imperfections.

'Look at me,' he commanded softly.

She obeyed, and her heart started to pound. Desire was stamped on his face and his eyes glittered beneath heavy lids. He stood up and came towards her, running his fingers over the diamonds nestling between her breasts.

'*Bellissima...*' he murmured, but she had an idea that he wasn't referring to the necklace.

He took the rose from her hair and trailed it down her cheek. The flower's heady perfume filled her senses and the petals felt like gossamer against her throat and breasts as he held the stem between his fingers and traced patterns on her body with the rose. He moved his hand lower, sweeping the flower over her stomach and thighs.

She did not know what to expect when he suddenly dropped to his knees and splayed his hands possessively over her hips.

'Oh...' Her breath hitched when his tongue licked along her inner thigh. 'I don't think...'

'Much better not to think.' He glanced up at her face and smiled wickedly. 'Hold on to my shoulders.'

And then his dark head was at the junction between her legs as he put his mouth on her and drove every thought from her head. Shock ricocheted through her when he pressed forward and ran his tongue over her moist opening.

He couldn't mean to...

But he did.

Heat swept through her veins as his intimate caresses grew bolder and the fire inside her became an inferno. It was too much and not enough. Pleasure bordering on something so needy and intense that it almost hurt. And the ache, the terrible yearning, built to a crescendo as Marco closed his lips around the tight nub of her core and sucked.

Leah cried out something incomprehensible as she climaxed against his mouth. Ripples contracted and released deep in her core.

Her legs buckled and he stood up and swept her into his arms. He strode over to the bed and laid her down on satin sheets that felt cool against her passion-flushed skin. She propped herself up on her elbows, wondering how she could feel so uninhibited at being naked, with her legs splayed open and the scent of her arousal in the air.

'You have too many clothes on,' she told Marco.

He shoved his thick hair off his brow with a hand that Leah fancied was a little unsteady.

'Another of my fantasies is for you to undress me,' he muttered.

Moving to kneel on the bed, she undid his shirt and pushed it off his shoulders. His muscles rippled beneath her fingers as she explored his powerful biceps and then placed her hands on his chest and felt the uneven thud of his heart. Following the dark hair on his flat abdomen to the waistband of his trousers, she freed the button and hesitated for a fraction of a second before running the zip down.

Her knuckles brushed against the hard length of him, making him swear softly.

'Witch... I'm enjoying this too much. And I don't want to risk disgracing myself or disappointing you,' he said gruffly as he pushed her hands away and finished undressing himself.

Her mouth dried and her eyes widened as he pulled off his boxers and his erection sprang free, proud and thick.

Marco gave a low laugh. 'Keep staring at me like that, *cara*, and this will be over embarrassingly quickly.'

'You're beautiful.' She blurted the words out and blushed, mortified that she sounded so gauche.

But his body was incredible: a broad, bronzed chest, an impressive six-pack, a taut torso and lean hips. Her gaze was drawn inexorably to his arousal, and she felt a melting sensation between her legs as she tried to imagine what it would be like to have that thick length inside her.

She stretched out her hand and touched him, startled to feel solid steel beneath satin skin when she skimmed her fingertips over his shaft.

'*Dio...*' he growled. 'You're killing me.'

She watched him roll on a condom. A nerve flickered in his jaw and she sensed the restraint he was imposing on himself.

'Are you sure, Leah?'

She was still kneeling on the bed, and instead of answering him she cupped his face in her hands and covered his mouth with hers.

At first he allowed her to control the kiss, but passion swiftly spiralled out of control and he eased her down so that she was lying on her back and he was positioned over her.

'Bend your knees.'

His molten honey voice quelled the faint jangle of her nerves. She caught her breath as he feathered kisses over her breasts before he sucked on one nipple and then the other, until she was aware of nothing but fire and need and a powerful womanly urgency for him to possess her.

She brought her legs up so that her pelvis was flush

against his. Marco pressed forward and she felt his swollen tip rub against her opening. His hand slipped between their bodies, so that he could guide himself into her slick heat. Slowly, surely, he eased inside her and paused, his brow resting against hers as she twisted her hips and her internal muscles stretched to accommodate him.

'Am I hurting you?'

'No.'

There was no pain—just a delicious heaviness in her pelvis and a sense of completeness. She gave an experimental wriggle and heard Marco exhale a ragged breath.

'It feels good,' she whispered.

'This is just the beginning, *cara*.'

He claimed her lips again, and there was an unexpected tenderness in his kiss that tied her heart in knots. And then he moved, effecting a deep thrust that drove the air from her lungs as he filled her. And then there was only him inside her, around her, his male scent intoxicating her, his breath mingling with hers.

He set a rhythm that was impossible to resist. Every thrust of his steely hardness created a wonderful friction in her molten core. Leah dug her fingers into his shoulders and hung on tight as the storm inside her built and grew ever stronger.

Marco slid his hands beneath her bottom and lifted her, angling her so that his relentless strokes, in and out, felt that much more intense. She looked at his face and wondered anew at the stark beauty of his features. The dull flush on his cheekbones and the silver gleam in his eyes told her that this was good for him too. Although 'good' did not come near to describing the exquisite sensations rolling through her, wave after wave, so that it was impossible to control her thundering heart.

It couldn't last.

She arched her hips to meet the bold thrust of his and he held her there, poised on the edge of an unknown place that she was desperate to reach. *So* desperate. Her breath came in harsh pants, as if she'd run a marathon, and her body trembled and shook.

'Now!' he said thickly, before he covered her mouth with his.

Her sharp cry was lost in his kiss as something inside her snapped, and the drenching, sweet pleasure of her orgasm was so intense that she wondered how she could possibly survive it.

Impossibly, it wasn't over.

Marco muttered something in Italian that might have been a curse or a prayer, increasing his pace with a new urgency that made her realise how much he'd had himself under control—until now. He thrust the deepest yet and threw his head back, his harsh groan reverberating through Leah as she climaxed again, swift and sharp this time, while he collapsed on top of her and pressed his lips to her neck.

For a long time afterwards he lay lax on top of her, and she relished his weight pressing her into the mattress. There was a sense of security in the arms holding her, in his fingers playing idly with her hair. She pressed her face against his shoulder and hoped he wasn't aware of the tears that trickled from the corners of her eyes.

He had made her first time amazing. The physical experience of making love with Marco had been mind-blowing. But she hadn't expected it to make such an impact on her heart. In those moments when they had soared together to the stratosphere it had seemed as though her soul and his were joined, just as their bodies were entwined.

But she would not get carried away with a romantic fantasy, Leah promised herself.

When she pushed against his chest he rolled off her and murmured something about dealing with the condom, before walking into the en suite bathroom.

Perhaps it was a cue for her to leave? She didn't want to appear clingy.

Swinging her legs over the side of the bed, she spied her expensive ball gown lying in a crumpled heap on the floor and, more damning still, the knickers that she'd discarded along with her inhibitions.

Swallowing the lump in her throat, she scooped up her clothes and hurried over to the door.

'Leaving so soon, *cara*?' Marco drawled.

Leah spun round to face him and her heart missed a beat at the oddly gentle tone in his voice.

'I told you…we've only just begun.'

'I haven't done this before. I don't know the protocol after having sex with a lover.'

Leah sounded defensive, and her green eyes were too bright. The faint tremor of her mouth smote Marco like an arrow in the centre of his chest and he rubbed his hand over the area above his breastbone.

'We are not lovers. I am your husband and you are my wife,' he said mildly. She was as edgy as a colt and he didn't want to spook her.

It was odd how much he liked calling her his wife. He would have sworn he did not have a possessive bone in his body. He told himself that this proprietorial feeling was because Leah was the only virgin he'd ever taken to bed. But he could not dismiss his satisfaction that she was *his*.

'I don't know what's supposed to happen next,' she muttered.

'Come with me and I'll show you.'

He held out his hand and refused to question why his heart leapt when, after hesitating for a moment, she put her fingers in his. He led her into the bathroom, where he'd already started to fill the circular bath. The hotel had provided an array of toiletries, and he added a liberal amount of scented bubble bath to the water.

Leah was clutching her dress as if it was a security blanket. He placed in on a chair and wound her long hair up, using the diamante clip she'd worn for the evening to secure her curls on top of her head.

'I've never shared a bath.'

Leah looked at him uncertainly when he climbed into the tub, scooped her off her feet and deposited her in the water. He turned on the jets and felt his heart clench when she let out a deep sigh as she slid down so that her shoulders were beneath the bubbles.

'This is heavenly.'

'It is a night of firsts, *cara*.'

Marco was fascinated yet again by the rosy colour that ran under her skin. She looked very young, with stray curls clinging to her flushed cheeks and her eyes enormous in her heart-shaped face. He felt fiercely protective and possessive and a host of other emotions he did not care to examine.

'I hope you were not disappointed with your first sexual experience.'

Her mouth curved in a rueful smile. 'You know I wasn't. It was wonderful.'

Dio! Marco was shaken by this unexpected emotional response to Leah. He tore his gaze from her lovely face and lifted the bottle of champagne from the ice bucket.

'Next time it will be easier for you.'

'Is there going to be a next time?'

'Would you like there to be?' He found he was holding his breath as he waited for her reply.

'Yes.'

He popped the cork and poured the champagne, handing her a glass. 'I propose a toast, Signora De Valle. To a fresh start.'

Her smile became impish. 'Mind where you put your foot, Signor De Valle.'

Marco put his glass down carefully on the side of the bath, not entirely surprised to find that his hand was shaking.

'Come here.'

He read the excitement in her eyes as she set her glass down and shifted across to him. She gave a gasp when he lifted her onto his lap and his arousal pressed against her bottom. Her mouth met his, and he loved her eagerness as she returned kiss for kiss. He gave himself up to a passion that had never been as intense with other women as it was with Leah.

This fire could not last, he assured himself, perplexed by the pang he felt at the certainty that it would burn itself out. Nothing good lasted for ever.

He rose out of the bath, taking her with him, and wrapped her in a fluffy towel before briskly drying himself. When he carried her through to the bedroom and laid her on the bed she sat up and gave him a shy smile.

'I have another fantasy...'

His breath hissed between his teeth as she moved down his body, her silky curls brushing over his abdomen and thighs as she put her mouth on his sex.

'Madre di Dio!'

'I'm sorry.' She lifted her head and her uncertain expression undid him utterly. 'Am I doing it wrong?'

'It's perfect,' he said hoarsely, tangling his fingers in her hair as she bent her head once more and licked along his throbbing shaft. '*You* are perfect.'

The still functioning part of Marco's brain acknowledged that he'd made a good decision to insist that their marriage contract was for a year. He'd done it because it would not look good to the company's shareholders if he broke up with his bride too soon after the wedding. But as his body shook, and he fought for control when Leah closed her mouth around the swollen tip of his manhood, a year did not seem nearly long enough with a wife who was more fascinating with every new discovery he made about her.

It had been a night such as he'd never experienced before, and Marco had made sure that Leah was as sated as he by the time they fell into an exhausted sleep.

He woke first the next morning, and propped himself up on his elbow while he watched her sleep. She was more beautiful that anything he'd ever seen, with her riotous hair spread over the pillows and her creamy breasts bearing faint red marks from his beard.

Marco pushed to the back of his mind the thought that he was behaving like a man who, if not lovesick, was dangerously close to it.

Leah opened her eyes and gave him the sweetest smile, and he assured himself that the tangled knot in his gut was simply desire. He had wanted her for a long time and now, finally, she was beneath him, her legs spread wide and her hips lifting to meet his. He tested her with his finger and found her wet and ready for him.

He reminded himself that this was all new to her and silently cursed his thoughtlessness. 'Do you feel sore?'

'No. I want you.'

She urged him down onto her, and with a groan he sank between her thighs and drove his shaft deep into her welcoming heat.

They finally made it out of bed late in the morning, and enjoyed a leisurely brunch in a charming café at the top of the Spanish Steps, with wonderful views over the city.

Rome in the middle of summer was thronged with tourists. 'We'll come back and I'll take you sightseeing,' Marco promised, when Leah told him that this was her first trip to the city.

He knew she was as keen as him to return to Capri to be with Nicky.

The days following their return to Villa Rosa stretched into weeks, but Marco barely noticed. His relationship with his son continued to flourish as Nicky's self-confidence grew and the trauma of the accident gradually faded for both of them.

Marco slipped into a routine in which he left early in the helicopter for his office in Naples most days, but returned to the villa by mid-afternoon. Leah taught Nicky in the morning, and the three of them spent the rest of the day swimming in the pool or at the beach, or strolling around the winding, narrow streets of Capri.

Nicky loved to ride in the chair lift to the top of Monte Solaro, the highest point on the island, but Leah preferred the less hair-raising charm of La Piazzeta, the lively square in the centre of Capri which was a wonderful place to enjoy a slice of *torta caprese*, the island's famous chocolate and almond cake.

'This is heavenly,' she said as she and Marco sat in a café one lazy afternoon.

They were spending the afternoon without Nicky as he'd gone with Silvana the nanny to a birthday party for Silvana's niece's young son.

Leah popped the last forkful of cake into her mouth. 'I'll have to watch my figure if I carry on eating so much of this wonderful food.'

'You have a gorgeous body,' Marco assured her. He leaned across the table and wiped a smear of chocolate off her lip with his thumb. 'It's a novelty to be with a woman who enjoys food. Eating is a sensual plea- sure…like making love.'

He held Leah's gaze as he lifted his thumb to his mouth and licked the chocolate from it.

Her eyes widened and rosy colour stained her cheeks. 'Marco! Someone might hear you.'

He laughed huskily. 'How can you still blush like a virgin after what we did last night?'

His arousal was instantly rock-hard as he pictured Leah, bent over the side of the bath while his hands had roamed over her as he'd taken her.

She gave him an innocent look. 'Maybe we should go back to the villa so that you can remind me of what we did?'

Stifling a groan, he paid the bill and slid his arm around her waist, urging her to walk faster across the *piazza*.

'Something tells me you're in a hurry,' she mur- mured, her eyes alight with teasing laughter and an excitement that made Marco's heart race.

'I am very hungry, *cara mia*.'

It occurred to him that if anyone had told him a few months ago that he'd happily delegate work so that he could leave the office early and rush home to be with his teasing minx of a wife he would not have believed it. The company had dominated his life for more than a decade, but now he had discovered that the simple enjoyment of kicking a football around the garden with Nicky or spending a long night in bed with his wife meant more to him than pulling off a brilliant business deal.

As for Leah—her passionate and sensual nature had been a revelation. But it was more than just great sex, Marco acknowledged. He liked being with her. She had been reserved when he'd first met her, but trust had grown between them and she'd lowered her guard and let him see that she was witty, with a dry sense of humour and a kindness that he would miss when the storm she evoked in him finally blew itself out.

But his desire for her showed no sign of abating yet, and he'd decided to stop wondering when it would happen and instead enjoy the lingering days of summer with her before winter and cold reality arrived.

As they hurried through the front door of Villa Rosa Marco paused to pick a white rose, which he tucked into Leah's hair.

'I can walk,' she protested when he scooped her into his arms and carried her up the stairs.

'Not fast enough,' he growled, shouldering open the door to the master bedroom, which they now shared.

He rid them both of their clothes before they fell onto the bed, mouths fused together, his hands curving possessively over her breasts.

'See what you do to me?'

He lay on his back beside her and his gaze met hers in the mirror above the bed. Their reflection showed

Leah's slim yet curvaceous body, her pale skin an erotic contrast against the black silk sheets, her nipples red where he'd sucked them. His erection was thick and hard, and he groaned when she ran her fingers over the sensitive tip.

'I prefer action to looking,' she said, with one of those smiles of hers that did strange things to his insides.

And then she rose up and straddled his hips, leaning forward so that her nipples brushed across his chest while he guided his shaft between her soft thighs. She took him deep inside her and he watched their reflection as she rode him, her red hair spilling around her shoulders. She tipped her head back and her eyes were as dark as a stormy sea when they reached the plateau simultaneously and tumbled together into the abyss.

Much later, Marco padded out of the bathroom, rubbing a towel over his wet hair after his shower, and found Leah sitting on the bed wearing his shirt.

How did she look so goddamned sexy in a shirt that was much too big for her? he wondered, admiring her toned thighs where the edge of the shirt finished. It was safe to say that she wouldn't be wearing it for long.

He forced himself to concentrate when she spoke.

'Silvana called to say that Nicky is having a great time at the birthday party. It's good for him to spend time with children of his own age. Your Aunt Benedetta will see a big change in him when she brings her grandchildren to stay, and Nicky will love playing with Dario, Aria and Giovani.' She hesitated, then said,

'Nicky is doing so well—I think he'll be ready to start school when the new term begins. He won't need me to give him lessons any more, and I've been thinking I should start to look for a teaching job in England.'

Marco felt the unpleasant sensation of his stomach dropping like a stone.

'I did not bring you to Capri only as Nicky's teacher,' he said. 'You signed a contract stating that you will be my wife for a year. If we were to divorce earlier it would give an impression of instability in my personal life—which, as CEO of the company, I want to avoid.'

She looked away from him. 'Is that the only reason you want our marriage to continue?'

He shrugged. 'For Nicky's sake too. The psycho-therapist says it's important to maintain a sense of continuity so that he feels secure.'

'I wouldn't drop out of his life. I'd come back to Capri to visit him. But I have a career. My inheritance money won't last long, and I need to work.'

Marco raked a hand through his hair. 'With regard to the divorce… As the contract stands you will not receive a settlement, but I am going to instruct my lawyer to alter it so that you will be awarded one million pounds at the end of our marriage.'

Leah stared at him. 'A million pounds?'

'It will allow you to buy a house in London and pay for your mother to continue her treatment.'

'What exactly are you paying me a million pounds *for*?' she asked, in a sharp voice with an underlying note that Marco could not decipher. 'Sex? Do I earn a certain amount per night?'

'Don't forget the days,' he growled. 'You are always eager for sex first thing in the morning.'

His jaw hardened as colour flooded her face. He was stunned that she seemed to be throwing his offer back in his face.

'I thought you'd be pleased that you won't have to worry about money in the future.'

'Oh, I'm *thrilled* that you think I'm a prostitute.'

'*Dio*—I don't think that. I made the offer as a sign that I...'

'That you what?' Her eyes flashed dangerously.

Marco unconsciously rubbed his hand over the ache in his chest. He didn't know what to say. He cared about what happened to her and he wanted to make her life easier—frankly, it did not sound like a bed of roses. But he sensed that Leah wanted a different answer from him.

'I made the offer as a token of my respect for you.'

She scrambled off the bed and marched over to the connecting door between her room and his.

'You know where you can put your million pounds! I don't want your money, and you have a funny way of showing your respect!'

She stepped into the other bedroom and Marco heard a tremor in her voice when she spoke again.

'I'll stay for as long as Nicky needs me, but then I demand you set me free.'

The slam of the door had a ring of finality to it.

CHAPTER TWELVE

THE STAND-OFF HAD so far lasted for four days and nights, and Leah was determined she would not be the one to break it. She was bitterly hurt by Marco's offer to pay her at the end of their marriage. It wasn't only the implied insult in his belief that she would accept the money—it was his admission that the reason he wanted her to remain his wife for a year was to keep his shareholders happy.

She'd thought that they had grown closer these past weeks. The attraction between them was stronger than ever, but she'd believed there was friendship too.

She had mentioned looking for a job in England partly to test the waters and see if she'd imagined that he felt something for her. Marco had not lost his air of self-containment, but she'd hoped that he liked her a little and even felt some degree of affection for her.

Clearly, he did not.

And perhaps he wasn't a slave to their passion the way she was. Every night she tossed restlessly in her bed and stared at the connecting door between their rooms, willing him to walk in and sweep her into his arms. She missed his body on hers…she missed waking in the morning with him beside her. She missed him so much it was agony, she thought miserably.

To add to the difficult situation, his aunt had arrived with her three grandchildren. There was no time during the day for her and Marco to be alone, and they were both putting on an act of being happily married in front of Benedetta. Even the joy of hearing Nicky chattering confidently to the other children was bittersweet when she could not share it with Marco.

Leah walked into the lounge and her heart gave a flip at the sight of him in jeans and a black T-shirt that clung to his muscular chest. His hair was ruffled, as if he'd been running his fingers through it, and she told herself she was imagining that the grooves on either side of his mouth might be caused by the same strain that she was feeling. He was sitting on the sofa with Nicky perched on his knee, and the three other children were grouped around him.

The little girl, Aria, held out a photo to Marco. 'Who is that lady? She's pretty.'

'That's Nicky's *mamma*, who is sadly no longer with us. She was very pretty and kind and talented. She hoped to be a great actress, and I'm sure she would have been. She loved Nicky very much.'

Leah felt as though an arrow had pierced her heart, hearing the huskiness in Marco's voice. It should not matter to her if his heart belonged to Karin, she told herself. But the burn of jealousy in the pit of her stomach mocked her belief that she was in control of her feelings.

The truth made her tremble. She had fallen in love with Marco. And this time she knew it was real. The mild affection she'd felt for James had never threatened her determination to stay in charge of her emotions. What she felt for Marco was terrifying and utterly uncontrollable.

She swallowed when she discovered that he was watching her, and turned away from his speculative gaze, afraid that he might see the truth in her eyes. Her heart was as fragile as spun glass and he could easily shatter it.

'Benedetta said you wanted to see me about something,' she said stiffly.

'Tio Marco, can we tell Leah about the surprise?' Aria looked excited. 'You are having a special lunch in the summerhouse for your anniversary.' She sighed theatrically. '*We* are not allowed to come.'

'You children are going to have a barbecue by the pool.'

Marco stood up and walked over to Leah.

Her brows lifted. 'Anniversary?'

'We have been married for two months, *cara*. Surely you have remembered?'

He smiled and brushed his mouth over hers in a tantalisingly brief kiss. For his aunt's benefit, Leah told herself as Benedetta appeared.

'How could I forget?' she murmured.

Her stupid heart was thumping when he took her arm and led her out of the villa, and she was glad she was wearing a blue silk dress that she knew Marco particularly liked.

'I suppose Benedetta arranged this?' she said, as he ushered her inside the pretty summerhouse set in a quiet corner of the garden. The table was set with cutlery and glasses on a snowy white cloth, and an arrangement of heavenly scented roses made a stunning centrepiece.

'No—I did.' He drew out a chair for her. 'We need to talk, but we'll eat first.'

He could not possibly be *nervous*, she thought as he poured her a glass of wine before filling his own glass.

There was a selection of delicious-looking dishes on a trolley, ready for them to serve themselves. Leah took some salad leaves and prawns, but her stomach was tied in a knot and she only ate a few mouthfuls.

'I'm sorry I upset you,' he said, putting his wine glass down. 'It was not my intention.'

'Maybe I overreacted,' she murmured, trying to dismiss the hurt she'd felt. His apology meant a lot, and she wanted their relationship to return to how it had been. 'But I'm not interested in your money, Marco.'

'I know that, *cara*.' He trapped her gaze. 'Over the past two months we have become friends, I hope?'

She nodded, not trusting herself to speak. She longed for them to be much more than friends. And this was not the stony-faced stranger of the past few days. This was *her* Marco—the man who had taken her to the pinnacle of pleasure countless times, always tempering his passion with a tenderness that had wrapped around her heart.

Guilt assailed her that she had misjudged him. 'I'm

sorry I suggested that you were trying to pay me for being married to you.'

He reached across the table and linked his fingers with hers. 'Our talk of divorce made me realise that it is not what I want.'

'Oh?' Her breath was trapped in her lungs. 'You… you *don't* want us to divorce after a year?'

'No.' He stroked his thumb pad over the pulse that was thudding like crazy in her wrist. 'It makes more sense for our marriage to become a permanent arrangement.'

'It makes more sense?' she parroted, ice replacing the warmth in her veins. 'How, exactly?'

'I never planned to marry again.'

Leah remembered how his voice gentled whenever he spoke of Nicky's mother and felt a stab of jealousy. 'But I blackmailed you into it?' she said flatly. 'The truth is I would have helped Nicky even if you had refused to marry me. I was shocked when you agreed.'

'I was, and am, willing to do anything for my son.' Marco lifted her hand to his mouth and pressed his lips against her fingers. 'You have enabled me to build a relationship with him, and I've seen the affection you have for him. I want you to be Nicky's mother. Hear me out,' he said, when she tensed. 'We like each other, and we get on well. We can be parents to Nicky. He adores you, and we can give him the family we both longed for when *we* were growing up.'

Leah bit her lip. Pride demanded she must not let him see that his words felt like a hammer-blow to her heart.

'I'd have no objection if you wanted to work,' Marco continued. 'You do an important job and you would easily find a teaching post for children with special needs in Naples. But at some point you might want to have a child. It would be nice for Nicky to have a little brother or sister.'

Listening to him was like refined torture, Leah thought bleakly. She *would* like children some day. It was her cherished hope that she would meet the 'right man' and settle down to have the family life she'd craved during her own chaotic childhood. Now Marco was dangling that dream in front of her, but instead of a pot of gold at the end of the rainbow, it was an empty bucket.

She eased her hand out of his. 'What about affairs?'

He frowned. 'I am fairly liberal-minded, but not about infidelity. You will be mine exclusively.'

His eyes glittered, and Leah despised herself for feeling thrilled that he sounded so very Italian and so very possessive.

'I meant you. Would you have mistresses? Presumably you'd be discreet, so that the paparazzi and your company's shareholders didn't find out?'

'You have my word that I'll be a faithful husband. I will commit fully to you and Nicky and the children I hope we'll create between us.' He leaned back in his chair and gave one of his sexy smiles that ripped the breath from her lungs. 'Seriously, *cara*,' he murmured in a softly teasing voice that, if it hadn't already been broken, would have shattered her heart into a thousand pieces. 'I'm a good catch. Say yes and we can spend the afternoon in bed.' His eyes gleamed like molten silver. 'I've missed you, beauty.'

It was terrible how tempted she was. Marco was offering her everything she'd ever wanted except for one thing. He did not love her.

'I need to think about it.' The chair legs scraped over the stone floor as she jerked to her feet. 'It's a big decision and I need time to consider my options.'

He stood up and walked around the table. She thought she sensed a new tension in him, but maybe it was her imagination. It would be so easy to fall into his arms, his bed, his charmed life in Capri that could be her life too. But there would always be something missing. His heart would never be hers.

He was so close that she could smell his evocative male scent: spicy cologne mixed with something that was uniquely *him*. She held out her hand as if to ward him off when he lowered his head. If he kissed her she would be lost.

'I need to be sure I make the right decision—for you, me and Nicky.'

Something flickered in his eyes, but he dropped his arm and did not try to stop her when she hurried out of the summerhouse.

Leah walked through the gardens and sat on a bench in a secluded corner, but she did not notice the colourful flowers or hear the birdsong. Her heart was thumping as if she'd run a marathon and her breath came in short gasps.

Since her argument with Marco four days ago she had longed for them to make up. But now she realised

that they could never go back to their old relationship.
Either she agreed to their marriage being permanent
or she would have to leave. Both choices would break
her heart.

Torn by indecision, she eventually returned to the
villa and found her feet drawn to Marco's study. The
faint tang of his aftershave hung in the air and her
stomach muscles contracted. She stood by the window, which overlooked the pool, and watched him
with Benedetta and the children. The sound of childish voices and laughter taunted her as she imagined
having a family of her own—Nicky playing with his
younger siblings, Marco cradling their newborn baby
in his arms. The dream was hers to take, and she ached
with longing.

But what would happen if the chemistry fizzled out
and he no longer desired her?

Would she become bitter and resentful, knowing
that he would never love her as she loved him?

She had spent her life feeling second-best to her
mum's alcohol addiction. Her mum loved her, but she
loved alcohol more.

Choking back a sob, she turned away from the window. Her gaze fell on the photo of Marco's first wife
that he kept on his desk. Karin had been so beautiful.
Her ghost was everywhere in the villa, and the many
pictures of her were a constant reminder to Leah of
everything *she* lacked.

The designer dresses she wore to parties gave her a
veneer of gloss and sophistication, but she was just an
ordinary woman who had foolishly fallen in love with

an extraordinarily handsome and attractive man. She
had tried once or twice to ask Marco about Karin, but
he had retreated behind barriers that Leah understood
now she would never breach.

She sagged against the desk, tears filling her eyes
at the thought of saying goodbye to him and to Nicky.
Marco had been right when he'd guessed that she had
formed a strong bond with his son.

Glancing out of the window again, she saw Nicky
playing happily with his father. In a few months he
would probably have forgotten her. The kindest thing
to do was to leave now, with no emotional goodbyes
and no risk of Marco persuading her to stay, Leah
thought as she hurried up to her room.

It did not take her long to shove a few clothes into
her holdall and grab her passport. Writing a note to
Marco took longer, but she kept it brief.

When she went back downstairs, the maid was taking delivery of a huge bouquet of roses. Dozens of exquisite pink and white blooms tied with pink ribbon.
Perhaps Marco had ordered them for his aunt's birthday tomorrow.

The florist's van was parked outside, and Leah
stepped out of the house and spoke to the driver.

'*Si, signora,*' he said, not hiding his curiosity. 'I can
take you to the ferry port.'

Marco had left the children watching a film in the TV
room. They were worn out after an afternoon in the
pool. His heart had swelled as he'd watched Nicky
playing and heard him chattering and laughing with

his cousins. The change in his son was incredible, and it was mostly down to Leah.

He strolled across the entrance hall and discovered the bouquet of flowers he'd ordered for her on the table. His mouth curved upwards as he imagined her pleasure when he presented her with the roses. Pleasing Leah and making her happy was surprisingly addictive.

Picking up the bouquet, he ran upstairs and opened the door to her room, surprised to feel his heart thumping. She had asked for time to consider his suggestion that they tear up the contract which stated they would divorce after a year. He'd given her a couple of hours. Surely she would have an answer for him by now?

In truth, he'd hoped for a more enthusiastic response from her when he'd told her his idea during lunch. He had known she wouldn't be impressed if he mentioned the wealthy lifestyle that would be hers if she remained as his wife. Leah was the most unmaterialistic person he'd ever met. Instead he'd played his ace—her love for Nicky.

Her room was empty. He had already checked the living rooms downstairs—the only place left to look for her was his bedroom. Was she waiting for him to make love to her there?

Desire jack-knifed through him as he visualised her naked body reflected in the mirror above the bed. He pushed open the connecting door and his anticipation turned to disappointment when he saw she wasn't there.

The ominous sight of a folded piece of paper made

his stomach swoop. Jaw tense, he strode across the room and snatched it up from the dressing table. Leah's neat handwriting covered three lines on the paper.

Three goddamned lines—that was all he was worth!

His temper simmered, but in the pit of his stomach he felt sick with dread as he read the note.

Marco,

I appreciate your offer, but your reason for making our marriage permanent is not good enough for me to agree.

It's best if I go now, before Nicky becomes too attached to me.

Be happy.

Leah

The words 'be happy' mocked him. How the hell was he supposed to *be happy* when the only person other than his son who made him happier than he'd been in his entire life had disappeared, leaving behind a pithy note that might as well have been a coded message for all that he understood it.

Dio, he had asked Leah to be his wife for ever and he'd promised her his fidelity. What more did she want? If those things were not enough to persuade her to stay married to him…he would have to set her free.

He sank down onto the edge of the bed, feeling the sickness in his gut intensifying to a raw agony that he'd felt only once before.

He would never forget the day he'd gone to the house in Rome that he'd bought for Karin—on top of the multi-million-pound divorce settlement he'd agreed to give her. He hadn't resented paying for it, so that Nicky would have comfort and security, but Karin had gone. She had disappeared with his baby.

Initially Marco had been terrified that they'd been kidnapped. But the police had confirmed that Karin had emptied her bank account, and a neighbour had stated that she'd told him she was moving abroad.

Losing contact with his son had felt like a bereavement, and there had been times when his grief had been overwhelming. His gutted feeling now, finding Leah had gone, was an inexplicable emotional response. He didn't believe in romantic fantasy, and he had no idea why he felt as though his heart had been ripped out of his chest.

A shattering idea pushed into Marco's mind and crystallised into a certainty that stunned him. There was only one real reason why he wanted Leah to be his wife. But instead of being honest with her he'd asked her to stay in their marriage for Nicky.

The truth was that he wanted so much more. He groaned and pressed his hand against his breastbone, where the pain was savage.

CHAPTER THIRTEEN

THE MIST WAS a thick blanket over Bodmin Moor, and the rain which had been fairly light when Leah had left the village lashed her face, driven by a vicious wind that felt no pity for anyone unwise enough to walk out on the moors without a coat. She had not taken account of the autumn storms that blew in off the sea around the Cornish coast.

When she had boarded a plane bound for the UK a week ago it had been warm and sunny in Naples. Now Leah doubted she would ever feel warm again. Or that the sun would ever shine.

The sullen sky reflected her mood as she bowed her head against the relentless wind and huddled into the woollen wrap that the landlady at the Sailor's Arms had lent her.

'Be careful up on the moor,' she'd warned. 'It's easy to lose your way.'

Nancarrow Hall rose out of the mist, grim and forbidding. *Like its owner*, Leah thought. At least that had been her first opinion of Marco. But that had been before she'd realised that he'd buried his heart with his first wife.

Grief took a terrible toll. Look at her mum after Sammy had died.

If anything good had come from her crazy decision to force Marco into marriage, it was the fact that Tori was stronger and more positive than Leah had ever known her to be. She did not suppose that her mother was completely free from her reliance on alcohol. There was no magic pill that would cure that kind of dependency. But ongoing therapy was helping Tori come to terms with the past.

Leah now understood the desperation to escape the pain of a broken heart. For the first two days after she'd arrived in England she'd shut herself in her flat, crawled under the duvet and cried a river of tears. She understood the temptation to anaesthetise agony with drink or drugs. But she hadn't. She'd discovered a steeliness in herself that would not allow her to wallow in self-pity or rush back to Capri and accept Marco's flawed idea of marriage.

She deserved to be loved. And she had to believe that one day she'd meet someone who would give her his heart.

If only she could rescue her own bruised heart from a life sentence as Marco De Valle's prisoner...

She brushed her hand over her wet face and told herself it was rain, not tears, running down her cheeks. Pulling the wrap tighter around her, she began to walk back towards the village. The sound of footsteps behind her made her glance over her shoulder, and her heart stopped as a figure strode out of the mist.

'Madre di Dio!'

Marco's expression was thunderous as he scowled at her, his eyes gleaming like tensile steel.

'Why are you standing out in the rain looking like a waif and stray from a historical melodrama? Do you see yourself as Cathy and me as Heathcliff?' he asked sardonically. 'Perhaps you have come to haunt me?' His mouth tugged into a crooked smile that did not warm his cold, cold eyes and he touched his scarred face. 'God knows I'm an ugly enough brute to play Heathcliff.'

'You are not a brute—and you are certainly not ugly,' Leah snapped.

She was still reeling from his materialising in front of her when she'd believed she would never see him again. His mockery had stirred her temper. She felt alive for the first time since she'd left Villa Rosa—but that was the effect Marco had on her, she thought bleakly.

'It's not *me* who haunts you,' she said in a low voice.

'What does that mean?'

She shook her head. 'What are you doing here? Is Nicky with you?'

'He has stayed in Capri with my aunt. As to why I am here…' Marco shrugged. 'You are in Cornwall so of course I followed you.' While Leah was still trying to assimilate this astounding statement, he murmured, 'I have just come back to the house after visiting your mother at The Haven.'

'What? How did you know...?'

'I first looked for you at your flat in London. Obviously you were not there. But your neighbour—Gloria, I think she said her name was—told me that your mother was having treatment at a private clinic in Cornwall. You told me your mother has an alcohol dependency, and my housekeeper remembered that you had asked her for directions to The Haven earlier in the summer.'

'Quite the sleuth, aren't you?' Leah muttered.

'I was surprised that you hadn't told your mother you are married to me. She offered us her congratulations, by the way.'

She gasped. 'You had no right to tell her. I didn't want Mum to know that I'd had to marry a stranger so that I could claim my inheritance and pay for her treatment.'

'I assured her that we had married for conventional reasons.'

'Wanting me to be a mother to your son is not a conventional reason—nor a good enough reason for us to stay married.' Leah couldn't disguise the raw emotion in her voice.

Marco stared at her. 'Why did you rush away like that, without a word?'

'Didn't you see my note?'

He swore and shoved his wet hair off his brow. It was only then that Leah realised how heavy the rain had become. Marco's jacket was plastered to his body, and her curls were flattened against her head.

'What is the only reason you would agree to stay married to me?' he asked.

'The fact that you don't know says everything,' she said thickly.

'I think I do know. You have fallen in love with me—haven't you, *cara?*'

Heat scorched her face. 'I don't have to stand here and listen to you. It's over between us.' She swung away from him, and would have tripped on a grass tussock had his arm not shot out to steady her.

'Like hell it is,' he growled. 'You are my wife and I want you back.'

'Why?' Leah tried to pull her arm free, but he tightened his grasp. 'You don't want me!' she cried.

'*This* is what I want, beauty.'

He hauled her against him, one hand in her hair, the other caressing her jaw as he bent his head and covered her mouth with his own. He kissed her with a barely controlled passion that fired Leah's blood and made her heart sing. If this was the last time that she was to be in his arms she wanted to leave her mark on him, so that every time he kissed another woman he would remember *her* mouth softening beneath his and would taste *her* on his lips.

She tipped her head back to allow him better access to her mouth and wound her arms around his neck. He groaned and pulled her hard against him, so that her breasts were crushed against his chest and she could feel his powerful thigh muscles through the thin skirt that was clinging to her legs.

His hand on her jaw gentled and he stroked his

finger down her cheek, brushing away the raindrops and the tears.

'This is what I want, Leah,' he said roughly, when he lifted his head at last. He stared down at her, his eyes glittering beneath heavy lids. 'Your fire, your beauty, your unique mix of innocence and sensuality that drives me crazy with wanting you. *Always.*'

'But what you are offering is not enough for me.' She stepped away from him and it was the hardest thing she had ever done. 'You have my heart, Marco.' She could no longer deny her love. 'But I don't have yours because it belongs to your first wife. I know you are still in love with Karin.'

He jerked his head back as if she'd slapped him. 'I didn't love her. I *hated* her.'

'Don't lie.' She dashed her hand over her eyes. 'You keep pictures of her in every room at your house in Capri. She was so beautiful… I can't compete, but I won't be an afterthought in your life, always knowing I'm second-best. I can never replace Karin.'

'No, you damn well *can't*!'

Marco was staring at her, and the dangerous look in his eyes made Leah shrink from him.

He frowned and held out his hand. 'Come,' he said tersely. 'Before we both drown.'

She put her hand in his because she did not have the willpower to walk away from him. She was weak, she told herself as he led her through the gate on the boundary of Nancarrow Hall and across the garden.

As they neared the house she hesitated. 'I can't see your mother and stepfather looking like this.'

'They're not here. They're staying in Northumberland to be near James and Davina and the baby, when it arrives in a few months.' He gave her a wry look. 'My brother was always my mother's favoured son. The house has been shut up since they left and the central heating has packed up,' he explained when they entered the chilly sitting room.

The embers of a fire were in the grate and he rebuilt it with logs and kindling. He struck a match, and soon yellow flames were dancing.

Leah drew nearer to the fire while Marco disappeared. He returned minutes later, wearing dry clothes, and handed her a towel and one of his shirts.

'Get out of your wet things and maybe you won't look so goddamned fragile,' he muttered, in a rough tone that curled around her foolish heart.

Ignoring his sardonic look, she stepped behind a big winged armchair while she stripped off her sodden skirt and top and put on his shirt, fastening the buttons. When she returned to the fire he had brought a tray with steaming cups of coffee. She wrapped her cold hands around the warm mug and stared at the flames, conscious of the erratic thud of her heart.

Marco did not join her on the sofa. Instead he leaned against the stone fireplace. He looked devastatingly handsome in faded jeans and a grey wool sweater, his damp hair curling at his nape. Leah stared at his bare feet and wondered how she was ever going to get over him.

'I met Karin soon after my uncle died,' he said sombrely. 'Federico had been like father to me and

I missed him badly. Karin was beautiful, and viva-
cious, and I was lonely.' He gave a harsh laugh. 'It's
strange how you can have a full social life and plenty
of friends but still feel alone.'

Leah nodded but did not speak, afraid to interrupt
Marco now that he was finally opening up.

When it's too late, she thought, biting her lip.

'Soon after we started our affair Karin told me she
was pregnant. I wanted my child so I married her.
But cracks had already appeared in our relationship,'
he said.

Leah gave him a startled look.

'De Valle Caffè was going through a difficult pe-
riod and I often worked eighteen-hour days. Karin
was bored, and after Nicky was born she left him with
the nanny much of the time while she went out with
her friends.'

He paused to stoke the fire until it blazed.

'She had ambitions to be an actress, and when
Nicky was a few months old she started sleeping with
a film producer. We decided to divorce, and I agreed
to her extortionate settlement in return for shared custody of our son. A week after I'd paid her the money
she disappeared and took Nicky with her.'

His jaw clenched.

'I employed private detectives to find her. The trail
led to Mexico, where her lover came from, but they
were never found. I'd given up hope of seeing my son
again when Karin contacted me four years later and
said I could visit Nicky.'

Leah put her coffee cup down and waited tensely for Marco to continue.

'They were living on a rundown ranch,' he said. 'Her lover had turned out not to be a hotshot film producer after all, and Karin had spent all her divorce settlement. She told me that I could have custody of Nicky, and take him to live in Italy, but only if I paid her ten million dollars.'

He grimaced when Leah gasped.

'I was incensed that Karin was prepared to sell Nicky to me.' Marco stared at the fire and when he spoke again his voice was strained. 'I lost my temper and told her I was going to fight her for custody of my son and she could rot in hell. I refused to give her any more money.'

He raked his hand through his hair.

'I went outside and walked around the ranch while I tried to bring my temper under control. When I returned to the house I discovered that Karin had driven away with Nicky. I couldn't bear to lose him again. I jumped into my car, praying I would be able to catch up with her so we could have a reasonable discussion about Nicky's future.'

A haunted look crossed his face.

'I drove round a sharp bend and saw Karin's car on its roof at the side of the road. She must have taken the corner too fast. There was a strong smell of fuel…' He swallowed. 'All I could think of was getting Nicky out of the car before it caught fire. I didn't make it back in time for Karin.'

'Marco!' Leah jumped up and went over to him,

her soft heart aching at the agony in his eyes. 'You were not to blame.'

'I know—but I didn't know it then. It was only later that an inquest confirmed that Karin had died on impact. I hated Karin for depriving me of my son, but she was Nicky's mother and I still wish I'd been able to save her.'

Leah touched the scar on his cheek. 'You risked your life to save Nicky from that burning car.'

He captured her hand and linked his fingers through hers. 'I keep those pictures of Karin to show Nicky. I tell him that his mother was wonderful and she loved him. He must never know that she was willing to give him up for money.'

His eyes narrowed and Leah attempted to ease her hand out of his.

'I had no intention of marrying a second time. Yes, I wanted to take you to bed, but I had no need of a wife—especially one who seemed as money-orientated as my ex.'

'No wonder you were so furious when I proposed a marriage deal,' Leah mumbled.

'But I quickly realised that you are kind and caring, and you established a connection with my son that I had been unable to do.'

'You were right when you guessed that I love Nicky,' she said in a choked voice. 'But even for him I can't accept a loveless marriage.'

'I didn't want to fall in love with you.'

Marco slid his hand beneath her chin and gently

forced her to look at him. The expression blazing in his eyes robbed her of her breath.

'I don't have much experience of love,' he said huskily.

Leah's heart shattered into a thousand pieces.

'Even when I suggested making our marriage permanent I was arrogant enough to believe that you were no threat to my barren heart. But then you left.'

'I had to,' she whispered. 'You offered me everything except the one thing I truly wanted. Living with you, knowing that you would never love me, seemed worse than leaving and hoping that I'd get over you.' Her mouth crumpled.

'Ah, Leah, my love,' Marco said quietly. 'When I read your note I realised what a fool I had been. I'd kidded myself that I was in control of my feelings, but you had gone, and the truth hit me. I wanted you to be my wife for ever because I will love you for eternity.'

He brushed away her tears with fingers that shook, and Leah's heart turned over when she saw that his eyelashes were damp.

'You have my heart and my soul, *tesoro mia*. All I ask in return is that you promise to love me and stay with me for the rest of time.'

'I will,' she said simply.

'Why are you crying, *amore*? I intend to spend every day of my life making you happy.'

'I *am* happy. But I'm scared this won't last.'

Marco nodded, and there was a wealth of understanding in his tender expression. 'It will. We have it all, my angel. Passion, friendship, trust and love. Always love.'

He drew her down onto the rug and they undressed each other with trembling hands. When he took possession of her mouth there was such beauty and promise in his kiss that the last of Leah's doubts disappeared. And when he made love to her it felt new and wondrous, because there was honesty in every caress and love beyond measure.

'*Tu sei la mia amata rosa,*' Marco whispered as he held her against his heart. 'You are my beloved rose. *Ti amo.*'

EPILOGUE

'IT WAS A lovely christening,' Leah said as she climbed out of the helicopter and Marco slid his arm around her waist, walking with her across the garden at Villa Rosa. 'James and Davina looked so proud of baby Sophie—and your mother is obviously smitten with her new granddaughter.'

Marco nodded. 'And Nicky seemed to enjoy spending time with his English relatives. It was James's idea to have the baby christened in Nancarrow Hall's chapel.' He looked down at Leah and his tender smile stole her breath. 'I'm glad we went to Cornwall to meet the newest addition to the family, but it's good to be home.'

Home. It had a wonderful sound, Leah thought as they strolled into the villa. It was early summer and the roses around the front door were starting to open, filling the warm air with their exquisite perfume.

'*Papà*, you promised we could go swimming!' Nicky ran up to his father, his big brown eyes shining. 'And Mamma too.' The little boy grinned at Leah. 'Will my baby brother like swimming when he's born?'

'I'm sure he will,' she said softly. 'When he's big enough you will be able to teach him.'

'Cool. He can have my armbands, because I don't need them any more.' Nicky tore up the stairs and paused to hang over the bannister. 'I'm going to get my swim-shorts. Hurry *up*, Mamma and *Papà*.'

'I don't know where our eldest son gets his energy from,' Marco murmured.

'Our younger son is pretty energetic too.' Leah captured her husband's hand and held it against the swell of her stomach. 'Can you feel him moving?'

Marco's features softened as he spread his fingers over her bump and the baby kicked. They both smiled at this sign of the new life they had created.

'Tesoro...' he said huskily, before claiming her mouth in a lingering kiss. 'In a couple of months we will be a family of four.'

'I can't wait for Matteo to arrive.'

'Have I told you how happy you make me?'

'Many times.' She linked her arms around Marco's neck as he scooped her up and held her against his chest, as though she and the child that she carried were infinitely precious. 'You make me the happiest woman in the world. I love you.'

His grey eyes gleamed. 'And I love you.'

* * * * *